Actress Zinaida Reich and theater director Vsevolod Meyerhold

Praise for

A Wedding Song for Poorer People

"[A] radiant and emotionally nuanced collection. … Each of these irresistible stories beguiles, captivates, and gives us a clear-eyed reminder of what it feels like to be alive."

—Lewis Robinson, author of
Water Dogs and *Officer Friendly and Other Stories*

"Alfred DePew packs these stories and novellas with the whole of human experience. Weddings and funerals, loneliness and desire, singing and dancing, love and forgiveness, art and murder and mayhem. His insights into the human condition frequently took my breath away. *A Wedding Song for Poorer People* is beautifully written, deeply engaging—and hugely, ridiculously entertaining."

—Monica Wood, author of
When We Were the Kennedys and *Ernie's Ark*

"DePew is a master of dialogue, conversations tense with longing and silence … These stories suggest that no matter how connected one is to one's purpose, … what pulls us in and out of safety is what another demands of us—what we can or cannot give …"

—Susan Stenson, author of
Could Love a Man and *Nobody Move*

"Alfred DePew can do no wrong in this collection of stories as he … takes up the age-old question of the purpose and power of art. … DePew is a master of the gentle satire, of irony and desert-dry wit, … *A Wedding Song for Poorer People* is a book of crazy wisdom, filled to the brim with laughter, generosity, and grace."

—Agnes Bushell, author of
The Enumerator and *Local Deities*

Praise for
The Melancholy of Departure
winner of the Flannery O'Connor Award for Short Fiction

"Lush and sophisticated. Heart and mind. Near and far-reaching. Stories that live longer than the duration of your reading them. Stories that live on after the book is closed. No fuller, finer fiction exists anywhere. This is literature. The gift."

—Carolyn Chute, author of
The Beans of Egypt, Maine

"Sensitive studies of loss and survival."

—*New York Times Book Review*

"DePew has impressive skills at hair-down narration and offhand wisdoms."

—*Kirkus Reviews*

ALSO BY ALFRED DEPEW

The Melancholy of Departure

Wild & Woolly: A Journal Keeper's Handbook

A Wedding Song for Poorer People

A Wedding Song

for Poorer People

For Scott

Stories by Alfred DePew

Best Wishes,

[signature]

MIXED MESSAGES PRESS

St. Louis

Published by Mixed Messages Press
A project of Left Bank Books
399 North Euclid Ave
St. Louis, Missouri 63108
www.mixedmessagespress.com

Ralf Waldo Emerson, "Give All to Love" quoted on p. 129.
"We'll Meet Again" by Hughie Charles and Ross Parker.
Copyright © 1939 (Renewed) by Irwin Dash Music Co., Ltd. All rights
for the Western Hemisphere controlled by Music Sales Corporation
(ASCAP) International Copyright Secured. All Rights Reserved.
Reprinted by Permission.
Bertolt Brecht & Kurt Weil, *The Threepenny Opera*, translated by Desmond
Vesey & Eric Bentley, NY: Grove Press, 1964.
Rainer Maria Rilke, *Die spanische Trilogie* quoted on p. 218.

Library of Congress Control Number: 2014953594
ISBN 978-0-9907680-0-5

Book and cover design by Achille Gardellini
Cover photograph: Public Domain. Photographer unknown.
Source: http://teatre.com.ua/

Printed in the United States of America

For Christopher Richards
and Chen Sun Campbell,
incomparable friends
whose blessings still sustain me.

And for Harry James Cargas,
teacher, scholar, mentor,
and post-Auschwitz Catholic,
who continues to fight
the good fight
from the Great Beyond.

Contents

Blind

THE FIRST TIME my mother was struck blind, she was performing one of my father's string quartets. She lifted her bow after the last note and simply held her hand out to the cellist, who helped her through the curtain calls and guided her offstage, where she sat quietly, her viola in her lap, and waited for my father.

She and my father adjusted so quickly, I found it hard to believe she really couldn't see, though her blank stare frightened me at first. More frightening than that, perhaps, was my father's concern for her, for I now realize how deeply shaken he must have been. All of this I picked up silently from my father's body, so attuned were we to each other when I was ten. As a teenager I lost this sense, lost his frequency altogether, and kept trying to find it again through his music. Now that I'm a grown man it has come back, and we know each other's mind without speaking in a way my wife, Miranda, still finds astonishing.

Soon enough, during these times of my mother's blindness, we would fall into our regular rhythm of rehearsal, meals, study, and household chores, the difference being that Mother wouldn't perform in public. I came to enjoy these times. Mother would dictate her correspondence to me, and I'd help her organize my father's tours and teaching schedule. Father taught me to cook, and we'd get so loud and silly that Mother would hesitate to eat the food we had prepared. Best of all, I got to take care of my mother's viola. I'd spend hours examining the wood, holding the instrument up to the light, peering inside to see how it was put together.

Then one evening, as my father read to us in the living room, my mother raised her head, blinked, and said she could see. Just as suddenly as sight left her, it had come upon her again. This happened several times as I was growing up. No doctor was ever able to discover the cause. "Hysterical" is what they called it, but there is not now and has never been anything remotely hysterical about my mother. The blindness followed no reason, no pattern of stress or upheaval. Not that there was room in our household for upheaval. There wasn't.

My parents prized order; their lives as musicians depended upon it. Even today, they rise at five and are in their studios by eight. When I got home from school, they'd have finished work for the day. We'd have tea and talk. Then I'd do homework, they'd attend to household chores, and we'd gather again at eight thirty for a light supper.

Not even my mother's occasional periods of blindness disrupted this schedule. Like my parents, I thrive on routine. I get up at five, careful not to wake Miranda, who works four evenings a week. I shave, shower, and take my dog, Stevie, downstairs to let her out. Then I make coffee, fix Stevie's food, change her water, and open the back door to let her in. Each morning I eat a bowl of granola with sliced banana and rice milk, or, in winter, hot oatmeal with almonds, raisins, and brown sugar. I'm always at my workbench by eight.

I make violas and cellos in what was intended as the front parlor, the largest room in our house. It gets the strongest daylight, which helps the varnishes to dry, always a problem in this Midwestern humidity. Most of the light streams through the bay windows that make up nearly the whole southern wall. The room can be closed off from the rest of the house, and I've installed a ventilation system that will be easy enough to take out should we ever sell the house. I've put down a slightly raised plywood floor to protect the original pine, and built shelving and storage spaces that stand up against the wall but can be taken apart and moved. A bright and orderly room: pots of glue, cans of spirits, jars of resins and gums for pigment in small labeled drawers; large cans of linseed and walnut oils; slots for my bending iron and cramping blocks; hangers for arching templates, files, gouges, planes, and scrapers. Everything in its place: That's the secret to a safe and efficient workshop.

Stevie sleeps in one of three or four spots, depending upon the season and time of day. In winter, she follows the sun. In summer, she hangs out under the shelves near the dehumidifier; she seems to like the hum of its motor.

Sometimes I listen to the radio. More often than not I work in silence, and as I gouge out the back of a cello, I hear scales emerge from undifferentiated notes. As I bend the sides, cut the front, and start to plane the surfaces, some notes take on more weight than others, rhythms and repetitions can be found, and a certain order establishes itself. I begin to hear the music this instrument will play when it's finished. And as I sand and rub the varnishes smooth with a cloth, I often close my eyes and hear Miranda's last performances of my father's string quartets.

Miranda came to us through my father's music. She played it in her first term at Juilliard and knew she had to study with him. That's how we met. After one of my father's master classes in Aspen. They were talking about Bartók when I walked up to them in the parking lot. What first struck me about Miranda was the strength in her upper back and shoulders. It took me weeks to realize she was only five feet tall. Something about her presence takes up more space than her body. She had her back to me. Her hair fell to her waist in a thick braid the color of cedar or cherry. I noticed the way it held light. My father saw me coming and held out his hand to introduce us. I wonder if he didn't have something in mind at that moment. He's always said he knew from the beginning that Miranda was the right woman for me. She turned, smiled vaguely. We shook hands. The strength of her grip impressed me, but she looked right through me, beyond me, into the air somewhere above my head, and turned right back to my father, impatient to resume the conversation.

When I saw her face, I knew. I'm not sure what I knew, but I sensed something about the whole story: strong jaw and nose, wireless spectacles that made her look older, the frown lines at the bridge of her nose, her lightly freckled skin.

When she turned her gaze back to my father, I felt a hot surge of embarrassment. I'd been summarily dismissed, and it got my attention because I knew she was important to me.

Miranda hung around a lot that summer. Clearly, she was enamored of my father, and she made herself something of a pest, which annoyed Dad until he sensed I was falling in love with her in my silent, awkward way. I was thrilled she was around, though she barely took notice of me, until we were back at Juilliard in the fall.

We started doing things together—I wouldn't really call it dating—and she began to turn her attention to me. I suspect Dad sat her down and had a talk with her in Aspen. He often had to do this with the young women who admired him, and if he let it go too long, my mother would remind him when she sensed a girl's crush reaching its crisis. I think Miranda was surprised to find she liked me for me, and not because I was my father's son.

"You're not anything like him, are you?" she said that spring. The fact is, he and I are very much alike, but we were talking about my decision to apprentice to a cello maker in Chicago when I graduated.

"Are you disappointed in me?" I said.

"No," she said. "I like it. And from now on, you can keep me in cellos. They'll be my only wifely extravagance. I promise."

This was the first I'd heard about marriage. The subject didn't come up again for months, but somehow, from that moment on, we were engaged. Miranda uses this as an example of my inattention to feelings, both hers and my own. Sometimes she's teasing, sometimes not. The truth is, I heard her say "wifely" and I knew what she meant. It's just that I was at the edge of the thought, and she had already waded into the middle and stood waist-deep in it, looking back at me. Once she had turned her attention to me, finally, she could see all the way in, and she liked what she saw, so she made her decision. Not that I hadn't. I had. I think I chose her the moment I first saw her and felt that hot urgency as she turned her back to me, as if I'd made no impression at all. It's that I didn't have words for it yet.

Miranda is swift in her decisions. She'll have a hunch, then a clear feeling, and that's that: She knows what to do. And she can articulate all the feelings and reasons right away. Even after eighteen years of marriage, it still annoys her that I'm slow and mute about my emotions. That's why it was such a relief, I think, for her to meet Frank. I almost wish Miranda were sleeping with Frank. I'd rather be jealous of my wife's lover than of her hairdresser, though Frank thinks of himself as a sculptor. He sculpts not only hair but a woman's whole being, the way she thinks about herself. Each session is a work of art, and he charges a small fortune, which makes it sound as if Miranda's hairstyle is more elaborate than it is. Her hair is short now; she cut it when she was in massage school. Every so often, she'll have Frank curl it or layer it. I'm careful to notice. I mean, I do notice; she's my wife. I like looking at her, even though Miranda often claims I don't see her, by which I think she means who she's becoming. And I'm not so sure I like who she's becoming.

You see, Miranda was a brilliant musician with a distinguished career. While still at Juilliard, she helped start a string quartet, and with them she traveled, made recordings, and taught. So her decision to give up performing surprised us all. One night she walked offstage after a Brandenburg Concerto and said that was it. She wasn't angry. She simply could no longer devote her life to music; she was going to be a massage therapist.

My father was irate, said she was throwing away a great gift, ruining her life. Miranda said she'd come to mistrust the whole enterprise of interpretation; she'd grown tired of the politics.

"Tired of the politics!" he said. "Poor child! The earth is made of mud! Grow up."

"But that's just it," she cried. "It's too intellectual. I want to work with something I can touch with my hands. I want to *see* the effect of my work, actually feel the body release what it's holding."

"Nonsense!" he shouted. He kicked over a music stand and stormed out. It's the only time I've ever seen my father lose his temper.

They didn't speak for six months.

I respect Miranda's work as a massage therapist. I do. Though I don't understand a lot about it, outside the purely physical aspects of stress reduction and general relaxation. I have a vague sense of releasing toxins from the muscles, but I've never really understood how it is that muscle tissue carries feeling and memory. The bodies we cannot see, the bodies of light hovering around the flesh, I comprehend not at all. But sometimes I imagine these bodies as music that collects around us and follows us throughout our lives, like fragrance. I suppose they're related, this unheard music and auras, but I've no idea how. Miranda's a fine masseuse, but, like my father, I miss her as a musician.

Still, she wants me to be more enthusiastic about her new interests, to react, to show my feelings more. She's convinced that my inability in this area can be traced to my mother's episodes of blindness. Miranda claims they were psychosomatic attempts to control my father. It's true Mother needed help getting around, but I wouldn't call her episodes ploys to get our attention. It's not really in my nature to explain the events of the world. I let Miranda do that. Women are the ones to examine the subtleties of relationship, not men. At least that's what I always thought.

Until Frank came along.

Frank goes beyond clairvoyant; he's omnipotent. His pronouncements cover every topic. Next to him, I'm a big dumb oaf.

"He's so sensitive," she says, "so aware."

"Which makes me insensitive and unaware."

"No," she says, "not exactly. It's hard to explain. You see, straight men …" She shakes her head. "Never mind."

When she still valued my opinion, she would ask me what I thought of Frank's proclamations.

"Frank says straight men never remember their dreams. You don't, do you? He says straight men only care about work and sex, their egos. Do you think he's right?"

Or: "Frank says it bothers straight men when women are assertive. He says they feel threatened. Is that true?"

How am I supposed to answer? It's as if my wife suddenly doesn't know me. I don't remember my dreams. I care about my work. I like sex. What can I say? Independent women don't bother me in the least; I married one. I was raised by one. My mother, blind, was more independent than most sighted women. I suppose, like most men, I often don't know how I feel about a thing at first. Days later, when I've had a chance to think and find the right words, Miranda will have forgotten all about it.

"Oh, that," she says, "are you still thinking about *that*?"

Or she'll add Frank's latest thoughts on the matter, which, to my mind, don't seem very astute. In fact, they're pretty much fluff.

"Well, of course you'd say that," says Miranda. "You're straight."

"So are you," I remind her.

"But you're a man," she says, "a straight man."

Am I supposed to voice every thought that comes to mind? Pretend to care about auras, hairstyles, past lives? Form strong opinions on matters about which I know nothing?

I imagine I could tolerate Frank better if he didn't hate my dog. I mistrust people who have no respect for animals. And Stevie knows Frank dislikes her. Frank's the only person I've known her to growl at—I mean, all the time—which is remarkable, given her history.

I found Stevie a few years ago when I was jogging in some woods beside the graveyard behind our house. It was fall, so I didn't think much at first about the rustling in the leaves, but it went on in a determined, urgent way. What arrested me was a steady whine, which had the quality of having already given up hope. I made my way into the heart of some brambles and scrub trees and saw this animal. I couldn't tell it was a dog at first, its fur was so matted. Her upper body rocked up off the ground, trying to free herself. She didn't notice me until I stood right over her. Then she reared away. She lay still, panting, and seemed to stare up at me. At first I didn't realize she couldn't see. I shushed her, bent down, and moved my hand slowly toward her nose. She growled, so I backed off and waited.

Her hind legs were hidden by leaves and branches. I was afraid she was caught in a trap. She kept up a slow, intentionless snarl as I lifted first one, then another tree limb off. When I'd cleared away the brush, I saw she was half buried, so I started to dig her out with my hands. The earth was hard, deliberately packed down. When I'd dug deep enough, I found a cinder block someone had tied her to. It took me a while to loosen the rope. Then I stood back to see what she would do.

First she pawed the ground and tried to stand up, but her hind quarters gave way and she lay back down again. Then she tried to sit, but she was too weak. I watched a long time to see if she might get up on her own, but she couldn't. I was afraid her hip was dislocated or her legs were broken.

Each time I approached, she growled. I kept talking so she'd get used to my voice. Every once in a while, I'd put my hand close to her snout, and she'd sniff me. It took an hour and a half before she'd let me touch her. Gradually, I took her into my arms and carried her out of the woods. She held her body rigid, trembling. From time to time, she snapped at the air around my face.

I took her directly to a vet who boarded her for about ten days. Soon enough, when I walked into the examining room, Stevie would hobble up and nuzzle my leg, so the vet was surprised when I asked her to find the dog a home.

"I thought she'd be yours by now," she said.

It's not that I didn't like Stevie; I did, a great deal. That was the problem. The dog I grew up with had to be put to sleep, so I had resolved not to have another dog. I couldn't or wouldn't see how much pain he was in. My father sat me down before I left for college and convinced me it was cruel to keep the dog alive. I was ashamed I hadn't seen earlier. I'd been too selfish and stubborn to give him up.

So I tried to find Stevie a home, but a full-grown blind dog isn't everybody's idea of the perfect pet, and I'd grown attached to her. Miranda said it was as if Stevie had chosen me. In the end, I couldn't give her up. Miranda's the one who started to call her Stevie, after Stevie Wonder. In this household it was important she be named after a musician.

Though blind, Stevie looks right at you. Her eyes seem focused and expressive, not at all milky. They look like big, dark marbles. The pupils are black with a thin rim of brown. In a certain light, her eyes are iridescent, like opals. There's a lot of life in those eyes; they catch you off guard for they seem to see. It bothers most people at first. Then they get used to it. But not Frank. In all the time Frank has been coming to the house, he has never adjusted to her. She seems to make his flesh crawl. When he does occasionally pat her on the head, he washes his hands right away in the kitchen sink, soaping them twice.

Two or three mornings a week, Miranda and Frank sit talking at the kitchen table. Neither of them begins work until early afternoon, and both work into the evening. Miranda rents office space from Frank in his studio in a strip mall across from Frontenac Plaza. Every wall is a different color, nothing seems to blend, and dance music blares from several speakers. Frank serves drinks on Saturday afternoons. So all these little old ladies have to shout at their hair sculptor to be heard over the music, some of them are half deaf at that age anyway, and once they've had a martini … Then you have Frank cackling and screeching as he dances from chair to chair, a curling iron in one hand, a tray of drinks in the other, his assistants all hopping around and clapping. It's quite a scene. You'd think it'd drive Miranda crazy, but it doesn't. Her room is soundproof, and she has a separate entrance. I think she quite likes stepping out into all that commotion from time to time.

I've learned to stay out of their way on the mornings they're in the kitchen. When I go in to get a second cup of coffee, Frank looks at me with a flat, fixed smile and all but holds his breath until I've passed. Miranda turns, says hi, reminds me that there's chicken salad in the fridge for lunch. Before I'm out the door, I see their heads bow toward each other, and their rapid, shrill discourse begins again.

It's not always serious. One day I heard screams and pounding. I ran into the kitchen, I thought someone was hurt, but there they were, wiping tears from their eyes, laughing.

"What's the matter?" I said.

"Oh, nothing," gasped Miranda. "It's just that Frank has this friend."

"*Fab*ulous," said Frank.

"Too funny," said Miranda. "I can't explain. Later."

She shook her head, shooed me away, and they were off again in peals of laughter.

One moment, Miranda praises Frank's superior sensitivity. In the next, what she really likes about Frank is that he's so catty. None of her women friends are anymore.

"Now that they're lawyers," she says, "all they talk about is work. And you can't be catty with straight men. They're not in touch with their feelings."   •

"What does that have to do with being catty?" I ask.

"Well," she says, "you have to understand feelings to know what might hurt someone if you said what you were saying to their face instead of behind their back."

The other day, though, it was serious in the kitchen. I could tell by how quiet they were. Sometimes Frank's moods are palpable; they fill the house. Frank has these depressions. The last bad one was around his birthday. February. He's a Pisces. Which according to Miranda has a bearing on the matter. He turned thirty and wanted to die. Because he didn't have a boyfriend. Because the clothes in the last *International Male* were all Puerto Rican colors. Because his aura was muddy, his chakras clogged. Because all he ever did at night was sit around eating Little Debbie Snack Cakes and watching TV. Because he was getting fat.

"Fat," I said to Miranda. "I've seen pencil lead with more heft to it than old Frank." He's six foot three and couldn't weigh more than a hundred and twenty pounds. When he crosses his legs, he can tuck his right foot in back of his left ankle.

"Don't say old; he's very touchy right now," said Miranda. "Besides, you know what it's like. Remember when you turned forty last year?"

The truth is, I don't. We had friends in for supper, drank a bottle of wine, and I fell asleep on the couch. Miranda thinks it was midlife crisis, what she and Frank say men go through. That I was numbing my pain. I say it's because I was tired and never drink.

"Oh, no," said Miranda. "It's deeper than that."

Maybe she's right, but I still can't imagine wanting to die.

And I'm beginning to think that makes me superficial.

Miranda and I never fight, but a few weeks ago, when I got up in the middle of the night to get a glass of juice, I stepped on something sharp on the kitchen floor. I thought it was a piece of glass. Then I lifted my bare foot and stuck to the bottom of it was—a toenail clipping: a broad, thick one with menacing little points at each end. I carried it upstairs and woke Miranda.

"Jacob, what is it?"

I just kept holding it out in front of her. She leaned over, squinted to get a closer look.

"A toenail?" she said.

"Exactly," I said. "I found it in the kitchen."

"And?" she said.

"Well, it isn't mine," I said.

"It's not mine either, Jacob. You don't suppose we have a burglar, do you?"

"Very funny."

"Jacob. It's the middle of the night. What are you getting at?"

"I get up in my own house, go down to my own kitchen in my bare feet to get a glass of juice. I step on something that nearly slices my foot open. What is it? A toenail clipping. Is it one of my own? No. Does it belong to my wife? No. It is the toenail clipping of someone else. Someone else's toenail clipping on the kitchen floor that I resurfaced by first ripping up all the old linoleum—"

"For God's sake, Jacob. It's a toenail clipping."

"My point exactly."

"What? What's your point?"

"Where did it come from?"

"Somebody's toe. The big one from the look of it. Couldn't tell you which foot, though."

"Oh, Miranda. Stop pretending."

"Pretending?"

"This clipping belongs to Frank and you know it."

"Are you accusing me of giving him a pedicure?"

"No," I said. "What I'm trying to say is ..."

"Yes?"

"Intimacy!"

"Give me a little more information, Jacob. I'm not sure I follow you yet."

"It's an intimate thing, clipping your toenails. A private thing. Something you do in your own home. Not in somebody else's kitchen, for chrissake. Not in the kitchen of somebody who is married to someone else. You're my wife. Cutting his toenails in my kitchen, our kitchen ... It's an insult!"

Miranda looked up at me for a long moment and then smiled.

"Oh, darling. Bless your heart. You're jealous."

Frank says if someone is especially sensitive to other people, the hair actually picks up—what?—invisible waves of sorrow that collect like so much psychic sludge. Frank's special treatment for this involves clearing the subtle bodies with crystals. That, and a good shampoo. He gives Miranda this treatment all the time because she tends to pick up whatever people release as she presses deep into their muscle tissue.

I wouldn't know about that. What I do know is that Miranda has remarkably clear intuition. It's part of what made her such a brilliant musician. I like to think music does the same thing as tension or sorrow. I mean, clings to the hair, so that it gets carried out of the concert hall and released into the air again when a woman turns her head suddenly and sees a pheasant in the park. Though it rises silently, it's still music and remains in the air a long time, years after it's been played, moves way out beyond our hearing, keeps traveling through time.

Miranda still plays. When I finish an instrument, she'll test it for me so I can hear how it sounds. One of the things I love best about the work I do is hearing Miranda play again, if only for a while. And once I get a sense of how, say, a cello sounds, I listen to her phrasing, the way the music comes through her. She sits in the large bay window of the workshop, a soft light on her face and shoulders. She raises her bow and brings it down over the strings and listens—we both listen closely—for any irregularities, any nasality. She nods, I nod back when we both hear the warmth and richness we're listening for. Her eyes close. She abandons herself to the music and to something else that may exist beyond the music, beyond either one of us.

I love Miranda. I love that she enters an unnameable realm, that she has this in her, and I cannot follow her there. I even love the loneliness of these moments and the ache of wanting to go there with her. I watch. It's a gift to be in the same room, listening, carried away by the music and back to Miranda at the window, her hair full of light—it seems to catch and hold it. Does her body catch and hold the light as well? She is deep, deep in that place I cannot know in her, and then I, too, am somewhere else, somewhere in me, and the sadness that lies in the gulf between these two landscapes is immeasurable. It moves, this sadness. It rises in my body as the sound rises out of the cello I've made, pours through Miranda, fills the room, carries me—toward …

"So. Was she really any good?" says Frank.

He stands in the middle of the kitchen. He's come to see Miranda, who's not home yet, so I've asked him in for a cup of coffee. Was she any good? How can he not know this was her life before he met her? Good? She was astonishing, one of the most gifted students my father has had in the last thirty years.

"Yes," I tell him. "She was." I put two mugs of coffee on the table.

"It's funny the detours we make along the path," he says, spooning brown sugar crystals into his coffee.

I take a small jug of milk out of the refrigerator.

He reduces it to that, a detour, her years of study, the hours of practice, the agonizing attention to details of phrasing, emphasis, color, the endless repetitions, all her brilliance and passion: a detour. How can I explain it to him? Then I know. It's none of his business. Private. Not something he deserves to know. And yet I want him to see this was her life, not a detour. As if I myself, this marriage, might be a detour on the path—to what? Frank? Pop psychology? Some kind of smug New Age spirituality? Giving people massages in the back room of a beauty parlor?

I offer the bowl of fruit; he takes a banana.

I want to smash his face. I don't know what comes over me. I've never bullied anyone. I'm not a man who loses his temper, but there's something about his smile, the way his eyelids flutter, what he insinuates. That Miranda's life as a musician was somehow beneath her.

Stevie trots in, sniffs, turns toward Frank, growls, comes to my side. Frank crosses his legs, tucks the right foot behind the left ankle, draws himself away from me.

"You know," he says, "there's this woman in Eureka Springs." He folds the banana peel and places it at the corner of the table. "She reads animals."

"Reads animals?"

"Yeah, you know. She's a psychic. You call her up and she gives your pet a reading."

"Over the phone?"

"Well, *yeah*. She's psychic, she picks things up. Like time and space don't matter, know what I mean? She's *fabu*lous. One of my clients has a pit bull she cured of submissive wetting."

"Submissive what?"

"Wetting. It's when you go to pet the dog, and he gets all anxious and pees on the rug. Which would be bad enough for a terrier or a poodle, but imagine this butch attack dog. Too embarrassing. So she calls this lady in Eureka Springs. And you know what it was?"

"What?"

"Guess."

"I really don't have any idea."

"Low self-esteem."

"What was the cure?"

"Tricks! Teach the dog tricks to make him feel better about himself. Now when someone comes to the front door, she has to lock the dog in the bedroom. He sounds like he's going to claw his way through the door and eat you alive. Next they have to work on his aggression. You should call her, you know, to see what's going on with"—he waves his hand once, as if shaking off excess water, toward Stevie—"your dog."

The back door opens. It's Miranda. Her eyes brighten to see us sitting together. Bonding, she imagines. But her smile fades when she senses the awkwardness between us. I excuse myself, call Stevie, and return to my workbench.

Once there, I hear the rise and fall of their voices as they pick up the thread of an earlier conversation. I'm adjusting a cello for a man in Chicago. An instrument changes over time, tunes itself to the player, remembers every note that's been played on it, wants to play in tune. A cello has memory and desire. I'm brightening this one up a bit; the cellist tends to darken the sound. Maybe Miranda has darkened in her years with me and Frank is the adjustment she needs to brighten.

As I work, I wonder what I'm not giving Miranda that she needs so much time with Frank. Can what he provides outweigh what I offer? My time, attention, livelihood, my body, love? What in her calls out for more? A shrill, nasally shout jars me. Snappish and aggressive. Frank's voice is like a violin with too much shellac in the varnish, which has permeated the wood and destroyed the sound. How does Miranda stand it? Unless time away from music has dulled her ear.

What am I not seeing here?

The question plagues me weeks later as I stand at the foot of Frank's hospital bed. The call came this morning. For Miranda. He'd put her down as next of kin. "She's out of town," I said. The nurse said he'd been mugged.

"How is he?" I asked.

"Oh, he'll make it. Pretty badly bruised, though. He's in no real danger, so we waited till this morning to call."

"What happened?"

"They don't know yet. Police found him in Forest Park and brought him in around three this morning."

I told her I'd be right over.

I'm relieved to find him asleep. It's Miranda he wants to see, not me. And somehow I know that Frank's life has been marked by just this kind of disappointment—that the one he most wants to be there never is.

The room is bare. It's too soon for there to be flowers or cards. Even so, I wonder where all his friends are. Given his talk, he's always surrounded by people. But maybe Miranda is it, there are no others. It's never occurred to me that he might be lonely, I mean really alone, and this might be what appeals to Miranda.

He's someone who needs her in a way I don't. Or don't show.

I stare at the swollen side of his head. The nurse has told me they're going to run tests, take X-rays to make sure there's no serious injury to the brain or kidneys. The right side of his face is a sickening purplish mass, and I remember how I felt when I found Stevie's broken, wounded body full of a wild fear that was keeping her alive.

What, I wonder, keeps Frank alive? Or me alive. Or any of us. And if it were me instead of Frank in that hospital bed, who'd be standing where I am now, watching me sleep? Miranda. My father and mother. Suddenly I know how Miranda will take the news of Frank's mugging; I can feel the outrage in my own body. And then the urgent thought: Don't die, Frank. For God's sake, don't die. Because it will break Miranda's heart. She needs you. It's as simple as that. And I need her. And I will never understand it, this friendship that feeds her in a way I never will. I feel a pain under my heart for all I'm unable to provide her, and I'm ashamed it's another man who fills this longing in her, ashamed we all have this need and sorrow that demand so much of our time, and now Frank lies here, the bludgeoned part of his face turned toward the light.

I move to touch his face but I pull back. What will heal him? What in him needs healing? Whatever it was that drew him to the park in the middle of the night, he wasn't expecting this, and yet he'd been willing to risk it to satisfy the hunger that Miranda cannot appease—something as simple and unremitting as sex.

I watch Frank sleep and, after a long time, I wrap my hand around first one and then the other of his long, bony feet under the blanket. When I close my eyes, I hear Miranda playing the first somber notes of my father's quartet in B-flat minor.

La Casita

1.

HENRY IS ONE of those Texans who's lived in Santa Fe so long, he sounds British. He likes to think of himself as a Medici—Catherine, most likely—in any case, a great patron of the arts. He's filthy rich. And to give him credit, he has impeccable taste and has been more than generous to me in the last fifteen years. So I shouldn't criticize. It's that I can't help but take pot shots at the way he lives—it's Palm Springs for this party, and Key West for that one, all the right gallery openings, all the right receptions. And here I am, living off his hospitality and his abundant, sunny good nature. I myself do not have an abundant, sunny good nature. I am more overcast with periods of sleet turning to snow.

"All right, love?" he said, starting the car, an old Mercedes station wagon, the color of buttercream, whose engine turned over right away, always assured of getting us wherever we needed to go, which today was from the Amtrak station in Lamy back to Henry's house in Santa Fe, behind which is a casita where I paint every summer.

"Yes, of course," I said, sounding more irritated than I actually was. Just tired from the three-day train ride. And each summer it takes me some time to adjust to being in the high desert.

21

"I got the panels for you from the lumber yard. The casita is all set up."

"Good," I said. "I'm eager to get to work."

"I got a new mattress for the daybed; it should be more comfortable."

"Excellent. Thank you, Henry."

I noticed he'd changed his hair somehow. No sideburns, and it was cut, part of it shaved, at a 45 degree angle up behind the ear, shorter than usual. And he was wearing a new cologne, one I'd recognized on younger men, and like the younger men, he was wearing too much. It put me in mind of gin … which made me thirsty, and it was only ten o'clock in the morning.

"I hope you don't mind sleeping out there," he said, "for the time being, at least. I have a full house."

Now Henry has five bedrooms, and I've never in all these years known him to have more than three houseguests at a time. I looked over at him. His eyes were steady on the road. He clutched the steering wheel; the skin on the back of his right hand was stretched flat.

"How old is he?"

"Who?"

"Whomever you've got living in your house."

One thin line of sweat inched its way out of the new haircut and down Henry's right temple.

"What makes you think—"

"How old is he?"

"Thirty-ish. Well almost. Twenty-*eight*. In July."

"I see."

"What do you see?"

"Never mind."

"Don't sit in judgment, Roger."

"It's not judgment so much as bewilderment. I've never under-stood—your life is a mystery to me. As mine is to you. We agreed long ago on mutual confoundedness. Let's stick to the agreement, and let it go at that."

"The truth is, I need your help."

"Nonsense. It's a midlife crisis. That's all they talk about on television."

"How do you know? You don't even have one."

"I don't need to. My students have spent more time watching TV in their eighteen to twenty-two years than I have spent painting in the last thirty-five. What they don't tell me, my colleagues fill me in on. And according to everyone, all you need is pills, though I myself would prescribe a good, stiff drink."

"I'm serious, Roger. You're one of my oldest friends."

Was I? Would I have said that about Henry? In a funny way, I suppose I would have.

"I need to get some perspective on this thing," he continued. "I can't describe it. All I know is I need your help."

"You toss me out of the house because you've got yourself a new boyfriend, and I'm supposed to help you?" I was a little surprised by how angry I sounded.

"Are you disappointed?"

"Try dismissed. Try *fired*."

"Fired?"

"Never mind."

We drove along for a time. I looked out the window at the sagebrush and dust devils and the mountains rising in the dis-tance. Red earth. Rock. The sky vast everywhere around. A big sort of nothingness that both shocked and pleased me to no end.

"You said you have a show coming up in November."

"That's right, November," I said, still looking out over the endless land. I said it in such a way that Henry knew the talking was over for now, and we drove on toward Santa Fe in silence.

2.

What I didn't tell Henry is that the show in November marks the end of my job at Claybourne College, where I've taught off and on for the past twenty years. I've been terminated, though the proper expression is "not renewed." "Fired" sounds too harsh and suggests something that could be contested by a lawyer. My three-year rolling contract has stopped rolling, and there's a national search for someone to replace me. Colleagues advise me not to apply, even my friend Mack, the dean of Arts and Sciences, though strictly off the record, to spare me the humiliation. By way of consolation—kind of a severance package, a muslin parachute, you might call it—they're giving me one last show at the college gallery. A retrospective. As if I were already dead.

What they're looking for is A) someone younger, B) someone with an MFA and not just thirty years of teaching experience and thirty-five years in the studio, and C)—here's the real one—someone who can do performance art. Perform performance art? Enact performance art? I've never been sure of the verb. I suppose it's simply to perform art, as you would an appendectomy. What they're looking for is any numskull who's too chickenshit to face what it is to paint and too lazy to be a real actor.

More to the point, my department—heretofore called Painting, but that's likely to change too—is afraid that if they don't hire a performance artist, and quick, the Sculpture Department will hire one first, and we'll be left out in the cold, a kind of postmodern nuclear winter. What's more is Mack has found the money (where do they always hide it?) to pay this person more than they are now paying me, so it's not even a cost-saving measure. It's an upgrade. You see we're not attracting majors the way we once did (neither is Sculpture, I might add), but when it comes budget time, Mack looks to the bottom line, and for the past four years running, he's found it floating somewhere above the Painting Department, which pains him, as he used to be a painter himself.

We are not, we are told, pulling our weight.

We are not, as our department head, Mirna, likes to remind us, thinking outside the box.

Mirna is a tiny, birdlike woman who couldn't weigh more than eighty-three pounds and who suffers from some sort of anxiety disorder. Two years ago, she took to poking sticks through her canvases in order to—how did she explain it?—explore the dimensionality of the painting surface, and … It went on a good bit longer, but it never made much more sense than that. Then she took to sticking rocks on her paintings, but they kept falling off. "All the better," she said, as if it were anything but using the wrong glue. "The painting responds to its environment and fulfills its longing to have three dimensions," a longing, she insists, that all flat surfaces share. Books, she says, have partially fulfilled this longing because they can stand up on their own, unlike a Barbie doll, which cannot because of the way her feet have been formed by a toy company that is owned and operated by phallocentric men hell-bent on making her life miserable. Don't ask me what a painter is doing with Barbie dolls, except moving into the new and possibly more lucrative territory of installations.

The Barbie dolls somehow qualify her as a feminist, so she is invited to conferences everywhere, is never at the college to teach her studio classes, and everybody loves her, especially the English Department, which every semester asks her to speak to their seminar in literary criticism. Mack seems to love her too, even more so now than when he was a man. You see Mack is undergoing a sex change, but that's another story.

I think everyone at Claybourne College loves Mirna because the winters are long, dark, and snowy, accompanied by an almost constant howling wind. Everyone's real longing is to be anywhere else but Claybourne College, but there we all are, listening to Mirna deliver papers on unfulfilled desire. In other words, she speaks to their condition. Not mine. I seem to have forgotten all about desire.

Claybourne is a small, independent college of liberal arts nestled—that's a lie, it's more like stuck—on top of a bald hill overlooking a lake in upstate New York. It was started by the Methodists and was built to resemble a rambling English country estate, all stone and ivy and slate roofs. For a time it served as a lunatic asylum, and it never really lost the feeling. At the bottom of the hill is the town of Claybourne, a sinister little collection of bars, diners, three Laundromats, a hardware store, and a bowling alley. The only reason we have any students at all is that the college never shows the place past Thanksgiving, and the catalog only ever has one picture of snow—still and bright, a rarity—and one picture of the town, an aerial shot taken from five thousand feet.

Which has a lot to say for changing your point of view. I wonder how high up I'd have to get to look down at my dubious future to see it as anything but a disaster. By the end of next May, my teaching salary stops, my partial medical benefits stop, and my identity in the world vanishes. I'll be left to my own devices, which have always been pretty ineffectual when it came to making a living. I sell maybe three or four paintings a year. Henry tells me to raise my prices, to charge by the square inch, sort of like real estate, which everyone keeps reminding me is going up and up and up. I don't know. It feels like just another crapshoot to me. I charge a fair price, and I like my collectors. Some of them have become friends. Like Henry.

I suppose I've been stupid about business all these years. Teaching does that to you, sort of lulls you into a drugged state like the Tin Man, the Cowardly Lion, and Dorothy when they reach the field of poppies and all lie down for a nap. Something about the altitude of higher education makes everybody a little drowsy, and nothing wakes us up like the prospect of a swift decent to the planet Earth. We'll do anything to escape that fate, and it usually takes the form of a Guggenheim or an NEA grant or refuge in some artists' colony for three months or however long they'll have us, sort of like hiking to a higher peak to camp for a year or so. Or we make a lateral move, a sabbatical leave replacement somewhere—please God—in the Northeast, but maybe out West or, if worse comes to worst, Arkansas or Tennessee.

I seem to be opting for a giddy free fall, and though I hate to admit it, I've always imagined there'd be a safety net out here in Santa Fe with Henry. But the presence of this new boyfriend might change all that.

3.

Things looked different in the morning, after ten hours of sleep. I made coffee and stood looking out the studio door into the lilac bushes and cottonwoods that form the line between Henry's property and Mrs. Montoya's. Maybe I could make enough paintings this summer to keep body and soul together for eight or nine months. If they sold. But of course they'd sell. Why wouldn't they? I had galleries in New York and in Santa Fe and in Dallas. And there was Henry who always managed to generate interest in my work among his friends. How much real estate could I create in three months?

Henry thought I was a nineteenth-century painter when he bought those first two landscapes. I remember them: gray and mauve, early-morning mist rising from the shrubs at the end of a stretch of lawn with soft hills and the sky beyond, and then the sharp line of an oak tree in the foreground of one of them. Nothing flashy or loud. Henry says that's what drew him to my work at first. I actually mix paint instead of applying it right from the tube. A gallery out here tried them, my friend Kate showed there, so I sent them some slides, and then five small landscapes. They were so different from anything else in the gallery—a relief from all the vibrant, happy landscapes in the place—that people took notice right away, and once red dots appeared next to the first two, the other three went quickly and at twice the price.

Henry was curious about me, wrote a letter, and I wrote back. We corresponded all that winter, and then he invited me out to paint for the summer. I packed up everything I'd need for three months, and shipped what I couldn't fit in my 1972 Volvo station wagon. That was fifteen years ago.

Now mostly I paint the figure, and I had an idea for a series and a couple of portraits, all of which I could at least begin this summer. I wanted to paint Mrs. Montoya again, Henry's back-yard neighbor. They haven't spoken for years. He wants to buy her house, and she won't sell. She doesn't like Texans on a good day, much less when they mean to turn her out of her home.

She's sat for me a number of times, and we always have at least one good long visit each summer. She seems to think I'm okay. I'm from so far away, somewhere in the remote North, maybe even Canada. Besides, she says, I'm "real European" not Anglo. Which in a sense is true. There's not a drop of English blood in my veins, at least not that I know of. She says I look like a musketeer. It must be the way I trim my beard. She admires my paintings. We've been allies for years.

But this day I decided not to begin the figures. I wanted to follow color in a random sort of way, just get out the brushes and mix pigments and smear them onto a surface. I do this to warm up, never keep them, work on paper, throw them away, though sometimes I wonder what they'd have looked like, these abstract studies I've done over the years. And if I could sell them now ... but they're gone.

I poured another cup of coffee and began preparing a palette without much thought. I pressed the palette knife into the small mounds of paint in a sort of meditation. Then I turned to face the wall where I'd tacked the gessoed paper, lowered my shoulders, breathed, noticed where my feet were, rooted but not fixed. I dipped a medium-size soft brush into a concoction of deep blue, followed the line the brush made, noticed that it turned a corner before it reached the edge. Turned back to the middle of the picture plane. A nose. Not a nose. An angle. An angle of repose. Which made me think of Wallace Stegner, his automobile accident, and Santa Fe's hospital, and where I'd prefer to be seriously ill if I was seriously ill: Here or back in upstate New York? Isn't everybody out here just a little lax, a bit too casual? For serious accidents and catastrophic illness, wouldn't I rather be farther north, where the cold keeps people on their toes?

I followed the line. A shoulder. Not a shoulder. I jerked
the brush upward and rubbed it in place, then rolled it in my
hand, loosely, and enjoyed the mark it made. I took a clean
brush and then another, dipped one into black, the other into
yellow, one in each hand. I watched as a bright drip from the
yellow brush descended, hit the thicker black line below, and
followed it backward along the edge. It's the spirit that allows
it to move like this, at this velocity. Quick as the Holy Ghost.

I think about all sorts of things when I paint, other than
my failures both personal and professional, the oil bill, or the
root canal I have to have done first thing when I get back to
New York because time's running out on the insurance. Time
is running out, period. I think about age and grace and dying.
I remember my past in various ways, view the future with hope
sometimes, but more often with a sort of low-grade despair. I
ask myself more interesting questions than where the money
will come from after …

I've done a number of self-portraits over the years. I don't
show them. They're private. They comprise a record of med-
itations, an on-going examination of conscience. Once I'm
outside the making of them, they look like confessions more
than anything else. The sins of pride, envy, gluttony are all
there. Sometimes I make myself stand naked in front of a full-
length mirror and paint the whole shebang: round belly, sway
back, flat feet, and all. Oh … and of course vanity shows up
in them a good deal.

It's a curious collection. I began the practice as an art student—drawing, collage, weird photomontage—before I settled
into regular painting. In fact, the practice started with our first
assignment in Drawing One: a full-length self-portrait in the
nude. They did that sort of thing in art school in those days. The

purpose was to pitch us headlong into abject terror, so we could work our way out again—probably the most important skill a painter had to have. Nothing after that seemed so frightening. Of course we all idealized ourselves or made ourselves look grotesque, a kind of self-satire that in some verged on self-hate.

In my early self-portraits not only am I young but I was seeing myself in a young way. How can I explain? The distortions came from the intellect. I would emphasize this or that part of my body, sometimes consciously to prove a point or to get at some underlying emotion. Now, at fifty-five, the distortions are what I see, my body as it is now. And the face is always a mystery and a surprise.

I was thinking all that as I continued to move two brushes over the paper tacked onto my studio wall, when I could feel someone watching me from the open door. I turned to find a young man leaning against the jam, one foot crossed over the other. Long legs, a handsome, ovalish face, almond-shaped eyes like a Modigliani, and black hair. Though clean-shaven, his beard was heavy, and his forearms were dark with luxuriant fur. His arms were folded over his chest, and his right hand gripped his left bicep. He had long fingers and a quizzical, provocative look on his face.

I disliked him immediately, and I must have looked annoyed.

"Am I disturbing you?" he asked.

"No one comes to the studio uninvited. If you need to get hold of me, use the telephone. That's what it's for."

"I'll remember that."

"Good," I said.

It occurred to me that he'd been standing there for quite a while, sizing me up. Not, I think, checking me out in any sexual way, though he must have been curious to know just exactly

what the nature of my relationship with Henry has been over
the years. The young man was noticing most likely that I am
shortish, squarish, and stout, with thinning hair cut short and
a trimmed beard, which is what makes Mrs. Montoya think
I resemble one of the Three Musketeers, albeit a middle-aged
one, retired from active adventuring.

If I were polite, I'd have put down my brushes and gone over
to shake his hand, but I'm not, so I didn't. He made no move
to approach me, and I was relieved.

"You're a painter," he said.

"So it would appear," I said, extending the two brushes in my
hand and looking around the studio.

"I mean Henry's told me so much about you. I was hoping
we could talk. I used to be a painter myself."

"Used to be?"

"Well, actually I'm more of a performance artist."

"Ahhhh."

"I haven't hung around anyone who painted, I mean with
brushes, in a long time."

"I see."

"Oh, don't get me wrong," he said. "I used to love painting,
but it's, you know, so toxic and bad for the environment. Then
I tried acrylics, but—I don't know. I got frustrated."

"Indeed."

"I mean I want to say more than painting can say, you know
what I mean?"

"No. I don't."

"I mean it's like paint is so—I don't know—like *static*, and
I'm all about *movement*."

Here he started to move into the studio, stepping back and
forth, moving his arms, sort of running in place and cutting

to the left, then the right, like those drills we used to have to do in high-school football practice.

"I want something more interactive," he said. "Know what I mean?"

"No," I said, "but I'm familiar with the argument. Painting is somehow not interactive, and performance or even video is. I don't see it. There's all kinds of movement in painting. Visual movement. It's inward. It engages the eye and the mind, and by extension, the rest of the body. Making a painting is physical work. When I stand in front of someone's painting, I sense the movement in the painter's body, where he stood when he made those marks, how he moved his hand, his shoulder, his torso. I can feel it in my own body. Look at Max Beckmann, Lucian Freud, Francis Bacon, and tell me you're not interacting with the painting. You'd have to be dead not to."

"Maybe I'd feel differently if I'd had you as a teacher," he said.

And I could see he hadn't heard a word. He was trying to charm and flatter me. I could tell by the stupid smile on his face and the way he batted his long eyelashes at me. He was trying to seduce me the way these boys do; it's half unconscious most of the time, but not with this one it wasn't. This must have been exactly how he snared Henry, and I began to see why Henry felt he was in trouble.

"Maybe," I said.

"I'm Jayson," he said.

"Hello," I said. "Now I'll be getting back to work."

He turned to leave, then turned back again.

"Oh, but I forgot," he said. "I'm supposed to invite you for dinner with us at the big house—around seven thirty."

"Not tonight," I said, "but thanks. Another time."

"Soon, I hope," he said. "I want to talk more. Your point of view is so interesting, and I don't get to dialogue with older painters now that I'm out of school."

I smiled and waited for him to get out the door before I turned back to the mess I was making on the wall, picked up the brush with the yellow on it, and jabbed it hard into the middle of the page.

"Older painters," I said under my breath. "Fuck you."

4.

The first time I arrived at the big house, as Linton, or whatever his name was, called it, I was exhausted. I'd driven from upstate New York to New Mexico in a thirteen-year-old Volvo station wagon that kept breaking down along the way, so I was nearly a week late. I stood at Henry's front door with the address written on the back of a coffee-stained envelope, waiting. When the door opened, I was met by a tall, broad, gray-haired man wearing some kind of caftan or Arab lounging robe, a light beige with red embroidery at the open neck and along the hem and sleeves. He was smoking a cigar and two white standard poodles swarmed around him like a cloud, silent except for the clicking of their toenails on the tile floor.

I laughed.

Henry looked puzzled.

"I'm Roger," I said.

"I gathered that," he said. "What's so funny?"

"You," I said.

"Well, you've found us, so come in," he said.

And there I was.

The house is built around a courtyard in a U, and for the longest time I'd get lost in it. I'd head for the kitchen and end up in the library. The poodles, Duzzy and La Belle, sensed my dilemma, and from the beginning, they'd herd me back to where Henry was—whether I was going there or not. There was a lot to look at, and I'd get distracted by the extraordinary furniture, sculpture large and small, and, of course, the paintings. It put me in mind of the Isabella Stewart Gardner Museum in Boston, but Henry's house had a lot less clutter and was done in better taste. Of course I spent most of my time in the studio, which had a small kitchen and a daybed, but Henry always had a room for me in the house, where I'd come to get away from having to look at the paintings for a while.

And he gave dinner parties. Oh man, did he ever. There were people he wanted me to meet: old ladies in turbans and their bleached-blond muscle-bound escorts, retired bachelors from the Pacific Northwest, people who might take an interest in my work, some of whom became collectors and friends over the years. So I came to feel—I don't know—sort of ensconced, I suppose, and the thought settled in my mind that some day I might come here for good. For years it was barely there, this thought, but when I'd get fed up with my students or the interminable winters in Claybourne, I'd take comfort in thinking I could let it all go and fall back into one of Henry's luxurious sofas in the U-shaped *House Beautiful* home in good old Santa Fe with my studio out back.

It would have been one thing if we'd been a couple, but we weren't, which means I had none of the rights and privileges attendant upon the conditions of domestic partnership between two consenting adults in the State of … Marriage. The very idea made my flesh crawl. Not that Henry wouldn't have liked that, even pressed for it early on, but I wasn't very good at being homosexual, and it seemed like a terrible sham to fake it for economic security, though there are those who point out that I have happily prostituted myself to Claybourne College all these years. I disagree, but that's a matter for another discussion. The point is that just as I'd been lulled into passivity at the college, I'd been lulled into a similar state by having a patron, for that's what Henry has been, as well as a friend.

You see Henry is rich, indecently and shamelessly rich. All he does is manage money that was left to him by his grandfather, playing the stock market and then making a small fortune even bigger through real estate, one of his passions. He buys something, fixes it up—really it's amazing what he can do—and then sells it to people with money who lack the imagination (it's a sort of genius, I think) to do it themselves. And Henry's wealthier and busier than ever before. In all this, he manages to support a dozen artists by simply showing our work to his friends and clients.

Why, you might ask, have I never given him any money to invest? It never occurred to me, that's why. The stock market bores me. As long as I have a paycheck and a little money coming in from paintings, and I can pay my mortgage and the oil bill and rent a studio, I don't give money a thought. In other words, I'll never think like a rich man, which is what you have to do to become one. Besides, I've always been a kind of Fabian socialist, which ought to mean I could live quite happily with the contradiction of funding my political ideals with sound investments in oil, armaments, and the pharmaceutical industry. But I am closer in self-righteousness to my Marxist brothers who are having none of it, thank you very much, even when it comes at their own expense, so to speak. Not martyrdom in the Catholic view but a grim, self-depriving Calvinist bid at some notion of salvation I can only hope to find once I've left this world.

That's why Anne Sexton said Protestants sing so much—because we're not sure. Poor Anne. A priest once told her to look for God in her typewriter, and I've always thought that was peculiar advice coming from a Catholic, except he knew exactly whom he was talking to and knew that if all else fails, Protestants understand work. Make anything look like good, honest work, and we'll be the first to sign up.

I nearly converted to Catholicism after college, but I suppose painting became my religion. I know that's a kind of heresy, but it's always made me sympathetic to the priest who told Anne Sexton where to look for God. Heresy is, after all, what Protestants live, whether or not we admit it, and I have to confess that I've substituted the sacraments for pigment and linseed oil and scratching away at a surface all day, stewing and fuming over edges and proportion, color and character. There's most likely a special place in hell for those who've confused glorifying God's gifts—and there are those who argue that my nudes and portraits are far from glorification—and glorifying God Himself. If there's one sin I commit, it's that, and I commit it every day, and once realized, it is a willful turning of my back on the comforts and sacraments of the church. And for this I've been sent a particular torture: postmodernism.

5.

"He's what I've always been looking for," said Henry. We were sitting in my studio some days later, nine o'clock in the evening, a bottle of bourbon on the table between us. Thurston—or was it Linton?—had gone off somewhere. "A new talent I can help."

"You always did like that," I said.

"But it's more. I love him. He's the son I never had."

"You always liked that too."

"Quit now, Roger. This is different."

"You've said that before too."

"Will you be serious?"

"I am being serious. You started out to tell me what makes this one different."

"So stop interrupting. What makes this one different is …"

There was a long pause while Henry poured himself another drink. I didn't dare say a word. I waited. In another moment or so, he said, "He's a great lover. I'm obsessed. And he's driving me crazy."

"How so?"

"He goes out on me. He cruises public places. I'm pretty sure he's having unsafe sex. He takes drugs. I mean other than the marijuana we smoke. Sometimes he seems to be quite out of control. I'll get a phone call at three in the morning. He wants me to come and get him, says he doesn't even know where he is, and he's scared. And he should be. I find him in trailer parks with drug dealers. I'm afraid he's going to get shot or bring criminal elements into my life, afraid they'll find out where we live and know where to find him."

"Sounds exciting."

"You son of a bitch."

"No, I'm serious, Henry. I think that's the appeal. He excites you. He's unpredictable. You're always on edge with him, which is what you like about him. I think you nailed it: He's what you've always been looking for, a son and lover rolled into one, and you have all the attendant grief and worry that go along with being a parent. You can't have it both ways, Henry, being a daddy and being carefree as if you were peers and equals."

"But that's what I want us to be."

"How is that possible? The boy is twenty-eight years old—you were at least that old when he was born! Then there's the money. He doesn't have a dime. How could you be equals?"

"Why couldn't you have been my partner?"

"I made a lousy homosexual. I had the wrong clothes, the wrong haircut. I never liked Bette Davis or Bette Midler or even Madonna. And to tell you the truth, sex with men always kind of bored me."

"Thanks."

"Nothing personal. And there'd have still been the money."

"What difference does it make?"

"All the difference in the world. Always has."

"Well, it shouldn't."

"But it does."

"So what lets you off the hook, Roger? Why is it that you're never in the throes of love trouble? How is it that you can remain so aloof?"

"I didn't always. You forgot about Kate."

"I'm sorry. I shouldn't have mentioned it."

"After Kate died, I don't know, I had to choose a new focus and intention for my life. I'd always had a purpose and that was to paint, and losing that, I almost lost my mind. I had to choose painting again and agree that nothing would ever again dissuade or distract me from it—no personal affection or lust. It was an act of will, a vow I've taken. Or I'm simply neurotic, depending on how you look at it."

"I'm not like you. I can't live without a lover in my life. So what do I do, Roger? I'm miserable."

"There has to be a pill—don't you watch TV anymore?"

"Be serious."

"I am. Or maybe you could give Linton something when he's not looking."

"Jayson. You mean slip him a Mickey?"

"That's right."

"I can't do that; it's unethical."

"What happened to 'All's fair when love is war'?"

"*In* love *and* war."

"Whatever. Just give him something to calm him down. A tranquilizer."

"I can't believe you're suggesting this."

"All right, then. Have you tried talking to him?"

"Yes. And every time I do, he threatens to leave."

"Where would he go?"

"Oh, he says he has friends he can stay with. That's what scares me—that he'll end up with them."

"He's not a child, Henry. Not exactly an adult from what I've seen, but not a child, and you're not his foster parent."

"I'm obsessed."

"Clearly. The trouble is you can't make your obsession work for you the way I can mine. In a sense my livelihood depends upon my being obsessed. For you, it's all agony and suffering and excitement and sexual pleasure, which is a lot, when you come to think of it, but—"

"Don't you ever get lonely, Roger?"

"Yes, but it's nothing a romantic relationship would help. I'm a solitary. My primary relationship is with painting. Sure there are times I want to run, call the whole thing off, times I hate painting and think I've wasted my life cooped up in a studio, times I want to chuck it all into the back of a pickup and haul the whole mess to the dump."

"So you just sort of rise above it."

"I don't rise above anything, Henry. I place my attention else-where. And I fight the same battles people fight in relationships, but I fight with myself instead of a lover or a wife."

"Didn't you and Kate ever fight?"

"Yes, but there was something impersonal about our battles. They were, on the surface at least, about painting and spirit and belief—a kind of ethics and how to live."

"High-minded."

"Maybe. Or a dodge, an evasion. We were both painters, and so our relationship was always secondary to our real work."

"What about sex?"

"There was that, and it confused everything and troubled us. We enjoyed it, and then it was a distraction, sometimes a weapon we'd use against each other, and then it was more and more beside the point. Neither of us really lived there, somehow. I can't explain it. And yet there are moments, painting, when I have a feeling that must be adjacent to what you must feel for Jimson."

"Jayson. You're going to have to learn his name, Roger. I insist."

"When I'm painting a portrait, sometimes I see something luminous in the sitter, something eternal. I catch a glimpse of who they are beyond any distortions of pain or personality. I see for a split second almost the way God must see. And surely that's love. Isn't that what you feel for …"

"Jayson."

"Jayson?"

"Not really. It's more down to earth. I want a companion, someone to share my life with. What I like is the potential I see in him."

"You mean if only he didn't take cocaine or drool when he slept or say such stupid things in front of your friends at the dinner table."

"How did you guess?"

"You're not Pygmalion. You either love him the way he is or not enough, and then that's something different—not love at all. It's not your job to educate him or save him from himself. As a teacher, I see young people suffer. I remember one a few years ago who struggled with whether or not she had a vocation as a nun. She felt called to join a Buddhist monastery and was terrified. And rightly so. A commitment like that makes all others pale in comparison. She was nineteen years old and called by another voice to immerse herself in the world. What should she do? she asked. I had no idea. How could I answer? I told her to go where she knew best for the answer: her spiritual director and her meditation practice. 'But what if I still don't know?' she asked. 'Then just try not to lie to yourself,' I said. 'Tell yourself the truth, at least. Begin there.' "

"That's just it, Roger. I'm not sure what's true and what's self-delusion."

"At our age, we ought to have a way of knowing. We're not nineteen or twenty-eight or even forty anymore, Henry. You know what's true for you. You've known it all along. And when you choose to ignore what you know, it's out of vanity or fear. At this stage of the game, you know exactly what you want in a partner, where you're fooling yourself, and what about this relationship is self-serving. Now whether or not you act on any of that is another question."

"He has me under his spell. I'm bewitched, somehow."

"Then ride it out; you've been bewitched before."

"Not like this."

"Because you're afraid this is your last chance."

Henry looked at me a long time without speaking.

"So what if this is your last chance?" I said. "What if there are no more boyfriends after this? What if you accept that you're in another station of life, one of solitude and reflection? An elder. A mentor."

"That's what I want to be to Jayson."

"I wonder."

"Why?"

"Because a mentor teaches a younger man his trade, develops his gifts. If he were interested in design, maybe. But this kid is a performance artist."

"That's just it. I think he's really a designer. This performance thing is just a passing—"

"Ah ha! Gotcha! You're not even listening to what he says. He is who he says he is. You're trying to mold him into something he may not be. If you go on trying to control him, I expect he'll go on jumping the fence."

I stood up. My back ached and I needed to sleep.

"End of sermon," I said. "I've got a lot of work to do tomorrow."

"I still don't think I'm trying to control Jayson."

"And happily we have all summer to argue about it."

"Will you come with us on Sunday to the Biennial?"

"Oh, Henry, I don't know."

"Please. It would mean a lot to me."

"All right then. Sunday."

"Come to the house at two."

"Agreed."

"And Roger—thanks for being here. I really appreciate your advice."

"Even though I'm full of shit."

"Even though you're full of shit."

6.

So there we were at Santa Fe's first-ever Biennial, just the three of us, Henry and Jimson and me. For Henry's sake. To get to know each other, because supper at the big house with just the two of them was more than I could manage at this point. I had been in town for over a week, and word was out among the friends Henry and I have in common, so I had to show my face at something, and I can no longer abide the opera, which, in any case, didn't start for another month.

So there we were at the Biennial, at a panel discussion under a large tent. This is the way new work is showcased, said the panelists, for they spoke with one voice. The old museum and gallery system was elitist and patriarchal. This new work, they explained, had burst the bounds of what we traditionally think of as art (that would be painting). Soon enough the panel members sounded like what they were: fusty theoreticians with PhDs in cultural studies. The rhetoric had changed, but the sound was the same as always, a kind of drone.

Once inside the exhibition, my spirits lifted. There were lots of things to climb on and stick your hands into. Sort of like the Boston Children's Museum without the educational overlay.

Jarred and I saw the fur-lined gloves and bug-eyed glasses at the same moment and went for them like a shot. In a moment, we were both wading waist-deep in bins of colored foam-rubber balls. Henry didn't know whether to be pleased or … something else. Clearly he wanted us to get along, but maybe not like this. Henry's expression was curious, just this side of dismayed, like an anxious parent, so I decided to up the ante. I went after Jimson like I was going to eat him. He leaped out of the bin, and I took after him, roaring and snarfling, a cross between an anteater and a grizzly bear, making vile suckling noises.

We couldn't see very well, so we weren't running fast—we still had the bug-eyed glasses on. Then Jarred started to squeal like a locust, and this pleased me to no end. When I did happen to catch sight of Henry's face in my kaleidoscopic compound eye, I saw a hundred images of distress. Then I heard his laugh, a forced "Ha ha ha," when what he really wanted was to knock our heads together and drag us both out of the place because as all this was happening, people he knew were wandering in and greeting him and then turning to stare at us.

I picked up the foam-rubber balls and started throwing them at Jarred, who caught them and dropped them out of his ass like balls of shit, which sent the children around us into gales of laughter, alongside of which I could hear their mommies hissing "No" and "Stop" and "Put that down."

This was, after all, art.

I felt Henry's hand on my arm. I took my bug-eyed glasses off. Henry was as pale as a tight knuckle. He tried to push out what I guessed was another "Ha ha ha," but it sounded more like he was on the verge of cardiac arrest; there was hardly any breath left in it. I understood right away that the game was over, but Jarred was down on all fours like a daddy longlegs, playing with a group of children who'd broken away from their mommies, who were now looking to Henry for a solution.

In a low voice, tight with rage, Henry called out: "Jayson! That's enough!"

Jayson got to his feet, took off his compound eyes, and blinked. The children knew there was trouble, but not Jayson. He was utterly without guile.

"What?" he said.

Henry simply glared at him.

I was still catching my breath and knew if I laughed out loud or even looked amused, life as I'd known it for the past fifteen years was over. So I cleared my throat and started gathering the foam balls and putting them back into the bin.

A large blond woman with red-rimmed glasses as big as TV screens came marching toward us. I was sure she was a docent or the director of SITE Santa Fe or an undercover policewoman, but she burst out laughing and in a voice deeper than Henry's cried, "VONDERFUL. Thanks you. You're de first people to gets my verk."

"*Your* work?" said Henry.

"Ya, mine. And dis is vhat I'd always enwishioned and intented."

She clapped Henry on the back, which sent him lurching forward, then she stepped toward Jayson and gathered him into an embrace that lifted him off his feet—and though slender, Jayson is no small boy.

I was impressed.

Henry's face brightened. Really he was afraid of looking bad was all.

And now I could let out the laugh that had been gathering in me and starting to hurt. I applauded us and said, "We got it! We got it!" and cut a nasty glance to the mommies who were starting to look sheepish, yet still self-righteous. The children gazed up at them, ready with hundreds of questions for the ride back to the suburbs.

I checked Henry's face again and saw that the storm had passed.

Jayson turned to me beaming.

That's when I took them both by an arm and steered them into another room where four videos of people pressing their faces against glass were being projected onto four different walls, so we made shadows as we walked through. Which is closer, I imagined, to the kind of interaction the organizers of the Biennial had in mind: quiet, tasteful, nothing that interrupts social intercourse, the murmuring and greeting we were now engaged in again like normal people.

Henry's relief was palpable, and Jayson and I had formed a strong, unspoken alliance.

7.

"That's some stunt you pulled yesterday."

Henry stood at the open door of my studio. I was going to have to start closing it; everyone was taking liberties.

"Stunt?" I said, continuing to arrange my brushes and pour linseed oil into an old tuna can.

"I mean your romp through the Biennial. You might have caused damage. I was highly embarrassed."

You see what I mean about Texas British.

"The artist loved it. It was right to the point. We interACTED wiss da verk," which was not at all what her accent sounded like, but it was the best I could do. "Besides," I continued. "You want Jarred and I—"

"Jayson!"

"Jayson and I to get along. And now we do. Like a house on fire."

"You're up to something."

"Nonsense. But we'll have to talk about it later. My model's about to arrive."

"Not Mrs. Mon—"

"Yes. Mrs. Montoya."

"That witch!"

"Well if she is, you best not be calling her names, or she'll turn you into a spider or make it so you never get another erection."

"You're trying to drive me mad."

"Don't be silly. I always paint Mrs. Montoya. We've been friendly for years. You know that."

"Passive-aggressive."

"Call it what you like, she'll be here in a minute."

I put my hands on Henry's shoulders, noticed their strength and heat, and pushed him back out the door.

"We need to talk," he said.

"Okay, but not now. How about this evening? I'll come for supper."

"I mean alone."

"All right, then, we'll make a time."

"But come dine with us anyway."

"It's a deal. I'll come at six thirty. And Henry ..." He had started to walk back to the big house. He turned. "I need to enforce the Call Before You Visit rule. Okay? And tell ..."

"Jayson!"

"Jayson."

8.

Mrs. Montoya appeared not five minutes later. We kissed each other lightly on the cheek, and she settled into the one-armed chair. I fetched her a pillow so she'd be more comfortable. She watched me in silence as I started to mix paint.

"It's good to see you, Roger. I always know it's really summer when you're here."

"How was your winter?" I asked.

"Long. Cold. Dark. They're harder for me now that I'm older. And yours?"

"Longer, colder, darker than yours, but productive. I seem to thrive on it. Something in my nature loves bad weather."

"You live too far away, Roger. When are you moving to Santa Fe?"

"Oh, I think about it every once in a while, but everything's gotten so expensive. And I'd miss the coming and going. I like the rhythm of it, the change. If I were here year-round—"

"But you're not so young anymore. When are you going to settle down? Retire maybe."

"I am settled. In two different places."

"How is that possible?"

"I'm not sure I can explain. Let me think about it for a while."

We fell into another long silence as I made washes of underpainting, everything in complementary colors. Where I saw red tones, I put down green; blue, orange; yellow, violet. Mrs. Montoya sat at three-quarters view and looked straight ahead at the abstract studies on the wall.

At one point, I looked up, and she was unbuttoning her blouse, white with a lace collar. Her hands worked slowly, carefully on each white bone button. I gave her a quizzical look, then went on blocking in the larger shapes. When I looked again, I saw that where there should have been a mass of soft flesh, there was instead a white crescent moon of scar tissue. She left the other breast partially covered by her blouse.

"Paint this," she said.

"Are you sure?"

"Yes, Roger. I may be dying. Maybe not. But I want you to paint me as I am, the way you always do. And this is how I am now."

"Cancer."

"Yes."

"Do you want to talk about it?" I said, continuing to paint.

"Not now," she said. "I'd rather be quiet."

She sat for me until almost one. Something about her face, the moment, the light that made me want to keep going, yet I was concerned about her stamina. We took short breaks. I fixed tea. She caught me up on the neighborhood, her family, her own paintings, the santos and the bultos she could no longer carve because she had lost so much strength in her right arm.

9.

I wasn't much in the mood for supper with Henry and Jayson that evening, but I went anyway, feeling the weight of Mrs. Montoya's illness. I wondered if Henry knew, and if it made any difference to him, in the way he treated her. I resolved to tell him the next time we were alone.

Henry was poaching salmon. There was to be brown rice, green beans, salad. We were having drinks in the little Zen garden Henry had designed some years ago. It's laid out in such a way that it seems much more spacious than it is. There's a small brook running through it over stones, a fountain really, and miniature Japanese maples and irises. Smooth stones, intimate, peaceful, a world unto itself that I walk through to go between the house and my studio—*the* studio. Mustn't get too possessive here. The world is mutable, full of uncertainty.

"You're lucky," said Jayson, turning to me.

"How so?" I asked.

"Teaching, living in the East, painting, summers off, coming out here."

"It's not as easy as it looks," I said, glancing at Henry, who was looking dreamily at Jayson, "but I suppose you're right. I am lucky." And at that moment I really felt it. I'd had a good painting day, and as heavily as Mrs. Montoya's cancer weighed on me, something was already beginning to happen in the picture I couldn't have hoped for. I would lose it, of course, but maybe it would come back. At the moment, I felt astonished and blessed. In this state I could be generous and felt something like happiness for Henry and Jayson, though I was missing Henry's company, our endless debates with no resolution.

They were in the kitchen, attending to details, so I was alone in the garden I'd watched Henry create over the years, content in my good fortune, when I heard Henry's voice through the window.

"Honey, where did you put the wire whisk?"

"Isn't it on the counter?"

"No."

"Well, that's where I left it."

"Jayson, how many times do I have to tell you to hang it over the stove, where it belongs? Did you remember to get the dill?"

"They were out of it."

"How am I supposed to make my dill sauce without the dill?"

"Sorry."

"You might have told me."

"I *said* I was sorry."

Domestic disputes are the reason I live alone. Now they were arguing just out of earshot. Evidently they'd deepened into something more serious. I stretched and poured myself another gin and tonic. One of Henry's great virtues is that he makes gin and tonic by the pitcher. I stood up and walked toward the little stone pagoda when I heard something shatter.

Henry's voice: "How dare you! That was an expensive vase! From Milan!"

Jayson's voice: "So? It's an object. A vase. Chill out. You're so fucking uptight."

"Jayson, I've spoken to you about that language. Please. And you broke it. On purpose. You've destroyed another artist's work."

"All right. I'll pay for it."

"With what, may I ask? And that's not the point. It was willful, hateful."

"So I have will! I have hate!"

And out stormed Jayson, blowing air and shaking his arms out.

"What's with that guy?" he said.

"Henry?" I said. "He's fussy. Most designers and art collectors are. He has a passion for beautifully made objects. It's something like a religious feeling, I guess. I mean that's why the house is so—"

"It's like a museum," Jayson said with a groan.

I was suddenly offended on Henry's behalf. "True," I said. "And a good one. Trouble in Camelot?"

"What do you mean?" said Jayson.

"The honeymoon. Is it over?"

"Oh," said Jayson, "you mean between me and Henry? No. I like to get him mad sometimes. Make him want to punish me. Then when we have sex, it's like *fire*."

I must've looked surprised. The energy in Jayson's voice and the pictures he conjured in my head were beyond anything I'd have ever imagined about Henry. I held the pitcher of gin and tonic out to Jayson who waved it away and went over to the bar to pour himself a shot of tequila. I began to wonder if we were ever actually going to eat. I was hungry and resolved to excuse myself and walk over to the Indian restaurant not five blocks away if supper wasn't forthcoming.

"Here we are," said Henry, carrying a plate full of shrimp and cocktail sauce. He had about him that god-awful bravado that arts administrators adopt when everything is about to slide into the shit once and for all.

Jayson smiled. I noticed that he too was a bad actor, which probably accounted for his choice of career.

"So!" said the all of a sudden Mr. Jolly Henry. "How's your work going?"

Meaning mine. They were both eager to deflect attention from each other and the fight they'd just had in the kitchen. They both leaned in at me, fascinated, desperate to know how my day had gone.

Of course what happened in my studio that day was none of their business. Mrs. Montoya had made herself vulnerable to me. I wanted to respect her privacy, and yet if Henry and I had been alone, I'd have told him about her illness and urged him to stop bothering her about her property.

"Well," I said. "It's going well. And I'm still looking for people to sit for me." I didn't want to bring up Mrs. Montoya. And if they could deflect to me, I could deflect it right back.

"Oh," said Jayson. "I will. I'd love to."

Henry looked annoyed, but almost everything Jayson said tonight was likely to annoy him. He was in one of those moods.

I paused, looked at Jayson. I squinted. I considered, not thinking so much as trying to see what might lie under the surface, in his eyes, the set of his jaw, his long, loose limbs.

"Yes," I said. "All right. Let's try."

"What's your hesitation?" Jayson asked.

I laughed. "It has nothing to do with you, really. I mean it's hard to describe what I'm looking for because I'm never quite sure, even once I think I've found it. I'm not saying this clearly. It's not as though I look for any particular quality; it's that I look to see if I can see anything at all. I mean about one's character."

"Character?"

"Someone's nature, something perhaps about their story, but more who they are at rock bottom. When I paint, I'm in a state of inquiry, much of it unconscious, much of it about color and relationship and light. But in another sense, it's a way of wondering about who it is sitting in front of me. And remember, though I paint what I see, I'm not exactly a realist. I'm always aware that I'm interpreting, maybe even distorting. So in the end, I suppose, it has more to do with how I see than who you are. I mean you're not likely to look to yourself the way you look to me, which is a long-winded way of saying, a lot of people end up not liking my portraits."

"Oh, I do," said Jayson. "I've been studying the ones here in the house. I keep coming back to the one of the girl in the black leotard."

"Olga," I said. She was a dancer and couldn't have been nineteen when I painted her. "You remember her, Henry. Is she still in town?"

"Dunno," said Henry. "I seem to remember hearing something about her a year or so ago, but can't remember what it was."

"Amazing young woman," I said. "I couldn't stop looking at her. She had no eyebrows, she was so pale and so blond, and with her hair tied up in back, there was this expanse of forehead that just seemed to keep on going. So there was about her a smallness and a vastness at the same time. Didn't she marry— what was that guy's name? Cid? Sam? Seth?"

"Can't remember." Henry shook his head.

We ate shrimp and drank in silence for a time. Then Henry started to point out things in the garden that were ready to bloom, and soon enough it was time to go in for supper.

I was grateful that Jayson was so talkative; it let me off the hook. I could study the paintings in the dining room while I pretended to listen. I examined a small Agnes Martin, a series of white horizontals over subtle vertical washes, color just whispered through the broad white stripes. I've always liked Henry's dining room; it has the highest ceiling in the house with windows that look out onto the Japanese garden, so that it feels airy and shady and green.

As Jayson talked, I began to think how I'd paint him. There was something birdlike in his movements, their quickness, the way his head perched on his neck and turned at odd angles, the way he extended his neck—it was really quite long—and then his hand would swoop across the front of his body like a wing. A crow, I thought. He took a bite of the food he'd hardly touched. I knew I should say something, for I felt myself drift back to my studio, mixing pigments.

"So you went back to Washington," I said. I wanted to make sure that the conversation didn't return to me.

"Philadelphia," he said with a mouthful of salmon.

"Philadelphia. That's right," I said. "And then what happened?"

"When I finished my MFA, I went to New York, did a few gigs in performance spaces, but people didn't seem to get it, so I thought I'd head out to California, but then my friend Tim suggested Santa Fe. I came out here and loved it; everything's so art-friendly, you know what I mean? Then I met Henry, and the rest is history."

No, I thought, you are current events. I'm the one who is history.

"And do you perform here?" I asked.

"Oh yes," said Jayson. "Henry's gotten me into all kinds of places, and the response has been awesome."

Awesome, I thought, of course the response was awesome. It always is in this town. Nowhere on earth are there so many standing ovations, no matter what you do. And the less the good people of Santa Fe understand it, the more thundering the applause.

Jayson continued to tell us about his gigs, as he called them, and my mind wandered. I was free to look into the piece of green Italian marble on top of the dining-room table. I followed one maroon streak in the stone after another, encountering flecks of gold all along the way.

"Then I'd have summers off—like you," said Jayson.

He meant me. He'd moved on to the next topic, and I was following the veins in the stone.

"Like me?" I said.

"Yes," he said. "Teaching would give me summers off."

"Oh yes," I said. "It would. I mean it does. Teaching does that. Yes."

"Do you like teaching?" he asked. "I mean is it worth it?"

"Yes, on a good day, I like teaching. And is it worth it? In the long run?" I paused here and then was struck with an idea. "Oh yes," I said. "It's more than worth it. It's invaluable, essential to my life as an artist. It keeps me in touch with … young people … with the process. I'm constantly exposed to … new ideas."

Henry gave me a peculiar look, as if I'd suddenly started channeling. In other words, he knew better. He'd been hearing me complain about teaching for years. I was careful not to look at him and held Jayson in my gaze.

"Nothing better for an artist. Never mind summers off. That's just part of it."

"It's what most of my friends are doing now. And I miss—I don't know—talking to other artists about my work. It'd be like being in grad school all the time."

"Exactly," I said.

"All that stimulation!"

"You bet," I said. "In fact, Jayson—I don't know why I didn't think of this earlier—there's an opening in performance art where I teach. You should apply."

"Really?" Jayson said.

Henry's face blanched.

"You'd be perfect," I said. "The Painting Department has created a new full-time position for an MFA in performance. Of course you'd be teaching drawing and 2-D design, but your upper-division courses would all be performance, and you'd be designing new courses from the very start."

"Awesome," said Jayson.

"Really, Jayson, people think of Claybourne College as a sleepy little place in upstate New York, but I tell you, we're poised for growth and a real national presence that will be the envy of our sister schools. We have a … vibrant student body and a killer faculty of emerging artists and scholars. We're breaking down all the old barriers between disciplines." Poking holes in the silos, Mirna called it, and the image that came to my mind was of grain pouring out onto the ground.

"Where in upstate New York?"

"In the Adirondacks. Beautiful lakes, woods. Easy access to … Burlington, Vermont."

"Vermont," said Jayson wistfully.

"Yes, Vermont," I said.

"New England," said Jayson.

"Well almost," I said. "New York isn't technically speaking New England, but close enough."

"Hey, wait a minute," said Jayson, "isn't that where Mirna Lodge Pierson Smith teaches?"

"Yes, it is. You've heard of her? She's our department head."

"You actually know Mirna Lodge Pierson Smith?"

"Yes," I said, "we've been colleagues for nearly twenty years."

"Oh my God. I so love what she's doing with Barbie dolls. It's such a gender fuck. She's fabulous."

"Yes indeed," I said, "lectures all over, cutting-edge, the whole shebang."

"Dessert!" said Henry, standing up suddenly. He was clearly annoyed.

"Not for me, thanks," I said. "I need to get going. I'm for an early start tomorrow." I stood up and drained my glass of wine, a dry Chardonnay.

"How do I apply for this job?" Jayson asked. "When?"

"I'm not sure," I said, "but the sooner the better, I should think. I'll call Mack, our dean, tomorrow and ask him—I mean her—how he … she wants to handle it."

"Her?" said Henry.

"It's a long story. For another time."

10.

Mack and I have been friends since I started teaching at Claybourne. We went from being painting buddies to squash partners, and then he became my dean. It's a friendship that's meant a lot to me over the years, and so I … well … I reacted badly when he announced he was getting a sex change. I suppose I should have been more sympathetic, but it caught me off guard. We were getting dressed in the locker room one day after he'd beaten me mercilessly at squash. He was pumped up and feeling grand. That's when he announced his plans to become a woman.

"You're not serious," I said.

"I am," he said.

"But why?"

"I want to be with women."

"You already are with women, aren't you?"

"I mean as a woman. I'm a lesbian."

I stood there for a minute, my jeans in my hand, staring at Mack who was naked in front of me. Mack is a good six feet tall, two hundred and ten pounds, solid, hefty, hairy all over, I mean everywhere. He's always worn a full beard. He is descended from those guys in Scotland who throw telephone poles around for sport. And at the beginning of each academic year, he pipes the new students into the chapel wearing his clan's kilt and sash and socks and cap and that enormous fur thing that hangs over the crotch—the full regalia. My point is, you don't get much butcher than Mack, and the only reason we make such good squash partners is that I can still move out of the way, I'm a lot stronger than I look, and besides, squash is a game of strategy.

"This," he said brushing his beard with his fingertips. "This," he said, slapping his big hairy chest. "This," he said, sweeping his hand in front of his genitalia, "all go."

I stared at him. "Are you sure?"

"I start hormone treatments next month."

"In Claybourne?"

"In Albany."

"Does this have anything to do with Mirna?"

"Well," he said, "as you know, we've been"—I couldn't even

imagine what they'd been—"spending a lot of time with each other, and we've grown quite close. In fact, Roger, Mirna and I are deeply in love, but it's a love between equals, sisters. We want to live as much as possible outside of the patriarchy. A new paradigm."

"Mack! The woman's a shrew!"

"This is so much your own stuff, Roger. You've felt threatened by her for years."

"I'm not threatened. She's a terrible painter. A crackpot. And hysterical."

"She's moved on, Roger, grown and responded to the emerging cultural questions in fresh, new ways. The times demand a new visual language. You've never understood her."

"Because she is incomprehensible—incoherent is more like it. Those Barbie dolls! Who's she trying to kid?"

"Mirna is a serious visual artist. She's attracting notice from important museums both here and abroad. Her work is provocative, engaging. And she's an excellent scholar, publishing in the finest art journals."

This was going exactly nowhere, so I changed the subject.

"So what's the process? How long does it take? And—forgive me for being selfish—will you still be able to play squash?"

"Of course," he said, laughing.

But gradually the squash games went the route of our conversations about art. The more fascinated he became with Mirna, the less we had to talk about. I found myself sidestepping topics that had once been at the heart of our friendship. What's worse is Mack stopped painting. Even before Mirna came on the scene—so I can't blame her entirely—Mack just stopped. He had always been a passable landscape painter, and we had often gone out on painting excursions together. I liked his work, we visited each other's studios in the winter, and the conversation was always spirited and wide-ranging. We disagreed and even argued, but there'd always been a friendliness about it. We liked each other. It was as simple as that.

Now we didn't seem to. Or couldn't. And I wasn't exactly sure why. Except that Mack had stopped being a painter and was now just an administrator, making quite good money, I might add, but he had dwindled, somehow, from friend and fellow traveler to bureaucrat and theoretician—I almost said theologian—and a bad one at that. Flimsy, smug notions about conceptual art and what the masses needed to "learn." He sounded more and more sanctimonious, when he really ought to have been standing in front of an easel in a stiff wind, trying to get the light as it fell across the treetops onto the lake.

Nonetheless, I punched his home phone number and waited. He picked up on the third ring.

"Mack," I said. "This is Roger."

"Roger!" He sounded delighted. I remembered how much I'd always liked his deep voice and wondered how it would change with the hormone treatments. "How are you?"

"Fine," I said. "Fine."

"And your work?"

"I've made a beginning. I'm still acclimatizing."

"And Henry?"

"Oh, he's fine. He's got a new boyfriend. In fact that's why I'm calling. He's a performance artist, MFA from"—I couldn't remember—"someplace impressive, and he minored in queer and gender studies as an undergraduate."

"I'm interested."

"I thought you would be. And so is he. I mean he sounds to be exactly what you're looking for."

"What's his work like?"

I paused a moment. "Beyond words," I said.

"That's saying a lot coming from you. You hate this stuff."

"I'm not saying I like it, Mack, but it's just what you're look-ing for."

"What's it about?" he asked.

About. Here I was stumped. Of course I'd never seen it, but from hearing him describe it, I felt I had a pretty good idea. "It's about movement, the body. It's … ah … kinesthetic, that's what it is, downright kinesthetic. Dynamic—that too. And provocative."

"Provocative?"

"Yes," I said. "He seems to provoke almost everyone he meets."

"What's his name?"

"Oh Mack, you know how I am with names. Linton. Or Thurston. Milton, something like that. Shall I have him call you?"

"Yes, by all means. And tell him to send me a video and a CV."

11.

I was eager to get back to work on the portrait of Mrs. Montoya. She'd brought me a santo of Luke the Apostle. The small painting on a block of wood showed Saint Luke making a portrait of Mary. Behind him was a winged ox. I assumed that she'd brought it because Luke was the patron saint of painters and bachelors. But he was also born a pagan and one of the first converts to Christianity and a martyr. I wondered what she might be trying to tell me. I put it for the moment on the windowsill behind Mrs. Montoya and found that it wanted to come into the painting.

I noticed I had drawn Mrs. Montoya sitting in an awkward

position in the chair, not quite the way she was really sitting, and rather than correct it, I got curious about how it seemed to intensify the scar left by her mastectomy.

"Are you comfortable?" I asked.

She looked startled. She'd been daydreaming. She closed her eyes for a moment. Comfortable. She seemed to be trying to remember what that meant, or searching her mind for a Spanish equivalent. *Placentero. Desahogado.*

"You mean can I sit like this for longer? Yes," she said.

I wanted to ask her what she thought I'd meant, but sensed she wanted to return to whatever she was thinking before I interrupted.

Where would my own thoughts go if I were her, if I'd had a part of my body removed and were waiting to see if the cells had stopped going crazy and settled down to their normal routine. How could cells go crazy in the first place? Stress? Smoking? The unnamed and unnamable waste seeping into the water table from Los Alamos? Or the stuff that had been released into the air in those first days of our fascination with colliding atoms, all that crazy bright light?

Something about the whiteness of the scar threw the whole thing off. It was unrelated to anything else in the painting, and yet it was a part of Mrs. Montoya's body, a mark of what had been and was now gone, a new fact. But it looked like somebody else's skin, in part because it was so white. Then it didn't look like skin at all, this scar. It was more like some terrible plastic, but it was her skin. It had been stretched and sewn together or grafted from another part of her body and would continue to knit itself into place cell by cell. It was quite beautiful in its way, this sickle-moon shape rising from tiny puckers of toffee-colored skin.

But it threw everything else off, as if something had burned through the canvas. It ran counter to the look of distracted serenity on her face right now. What then was I seeing? "Paint me as I am now," she had said. Well, how was she? That's what I was trying to get at, but all I saw was a problem in composition, a sudden interruption of visual rhythm.

The scar disturbed me. I feared it marked the end of Mrs. Montoya's life. I imagined the surgeon hadn't got all of it, the cancer spilling into the lymph river, flowing under a scarred moon. The body as landscape. Mack and I used to wax poetic on the subject, until he adopted the new ideology, became disillusioned with painting and with the land itself. He'd grown weary of looking at it, could no longer see a meadow or a hedge or a lake. All he saw was appropriation, rape, the oppression of women. I kept thinking of Mack about to lop off his genitals, not because they were diseased but because they no longer fit some new idea he had about himself. And here in front of me sat Mrs. Montoya, scarred, fighting for her life.

I had the palette knife in my hand and was about to scrape off the area of the scar when I stopped. I couldn't decide. I felt I had to resolve this before going on. Or I could ignore it for a time and concentrate on another part of the painting, the line of her jaw, her left arm, the window where the santo of Saint Luke now sat.

What in fact did I see when I looked at Mrs. Montoya? Intersecting planes, shapes, color, value, light. To the sociologist, she was a woman of a certain class and ethnicity, with the generalized history of her type. To the feminist, she was a woman multiply oppressed by Hispanic men, the church, economic conditions created by Anglos. To the travel agent, she was local color. To the physician, an experiment, a pile of charts and X-rays, percentages and chemical mixtures. To the priest, she was a soul with questionable eligibility for heaven. To her sons, she was a mother; to their children, a grandmother.

But what was she to me? A woman whose history I barely knew, for all we'd talked. A widow, Henry's neighbor, a *curandera*, a healer, a devout Catholic, faithful, superstitious, a good friend. A fellow traveler, an artist, a carver of bultos, a painter of santos. A Hispanic woman of northern New Mexico who recognized something kindred in me—a deep need for solitude and privacy and God. A figure against a ground, a series of visual problems to solve. A painting I would one day put up for sale to pay the mortgage or buy oil for the winter.

"Let's stop for today," I said.

This is why Mack quit painting, I thought. Too much noise in his head—most likely the landscape itself had grown cluttered with voices, mind chatter, so he couldn't see it anymore, couldn't connect. For wasn't that it? Didn't seeing connect us? But to what?

"How's it coming along?" asked Mrs. Montoya.

"I'm stuck. Flummoxed."

"Flummoxed?"

"Confused. Lost. Too much to think about. I need to simplify."

"Can I see?"

I thought a moment before responding. "Yes, of course," I said.

She came around and stood before the easel, looking. She smiled and said nothing.

"Well?" I said.

"When you ride rapids on the river, you get quiet and focused and clear. Then you guide your canoe with not so much effort. You let the river work for you. Here, you're still struggling to get into the water, no?"

I laughed. "That's it," I said.

Then we both laughed, and I put on the kettle for tea.

12.

Mirna phoned the next morning at seven.

"So tell me about this candidate you've found."

"Mirna, it's seven o'clock out here."

"I know. This is important. I've got a lot to do today, Roger." I decided not to ask her what she thought I was doing, as if painting weren't enough, but then I wasn't doing committee work this summer. I was not a team player.

"And Marta seems quite enthused about this young man."

"Who's Marta?"

"Mack. That's her name now."

"Marta? You must be joking. Can't we just keep calling her Mack? It's a great name for a lesbian."

"Point number one: I never joke. You know that, Roger. Point number two: This is her choice. I think we ought to abide by that, don't you?"

"Of course. Of course."

"So tell me more about his—what's his name?"

I froze for a moment. I knew I had to get this right. Meldron. Thurston. "Jayson," I said. "I think it's Jayson."

"Do you even know him?"

"Of course I know him, Mirna. I wouldn't recommend someone I didn't even know. He's"—I hesitated a moment—"Henry discovered him. Everyone out here is wild about him, and you know Santa Fe."

"Mmmmm," she said, though she didn't know a thing about

Santa Fe other than what the art magazines said. "What's his work like?"

I paused again, running through the vocabulary I'd heard in department meetings for the past five years. It was like trying to conjugate a Latin verb—beyond me.

"Playful," I said, "yet provocative at the same time. Fffffresh … but sophisticated."

"What's it about?"

She had me there. "Oh," I said, "you know … Look, Mirna, I don't understand this sort of work. All I know is that he seems to be exactly what you're looking for."

"It's not just me, Roger. We work collaboratively. As a member of this department, you're a stakeholder"—I suddenly saw myself about to plunge the stake I held into her heart—"a member of the team."

"I'll get him to send his slides."

"Slides? I thought he was a performance artist."

"I mean video. His video and CV. I'll tell him to send the whole thing."

"One last question, Roger. Why exactly are you recommending him? You've shown no interest at all in performance and new media since these conversations began some years ago."

"True," I said. "Let me put it this way, Mirna. If his work got my attention, just think …" I thought it best to leave as much as possible to her lurid imagination. "Besides," I said, "I want what's best for the department and the college."

"That's very generous of you, Roger, under the circumstances. This can't be easy for you."

"As a matter of fact, Mirna, it's not."

"And so I appreciate your willingness to think in new ways about art and art education."

As always, it sounded like Mirna was addressing a lecture hall full of people. She even talks about the weather that way: We have before us the exciting possibility of a fabulous thunderstorm.

"I won't keep you," she said. "I must say I'm keen on seeing this young man's work. So please, yes, do urge him to apply."

I was all set to ask about the weather, when I realized Mirna had hung up.

13.

Mirna's phone call put me in a funk, a mood so black I couldn't even look at the portrait of Mrs. Montoya. What was the point? No one would see it; no one would really even give it a glance. What people wanted now was a penny arcade, a theme park. I felt pulled by the undertow of the world, felt it suck the sand from beneath my feet as I waded by the shore, a riptide that pulls even the strongest swimmers down and has its way with them. Don't resist, the lifeguards tell you. Let it carry you. Ride it out; then when it's over, surface again for more breath. Which takes an enormous amount of faith. Who's to say the riptide isn't longer than the breath? What if riding it out didn't work and you drowned while waiting? Wasn't it best to keep kicking and fighting, so at least you'd expire while still flailing away—as if you knew what you were up against?

Mirna made me tired. She made me miss Mack and Kate and the two or three others in Claybourne whom I had liked talking to. Now there was no one, really, and I was exhausted by the interminable meetings about budgets and changing demographics and student retention. Maybe it wasn't despair that had driven Kate to suicide. Maybe it was simply fatigue.

And yet here I was out of bed, dressed, ready to paint—out of spite if nothing else. I would not hold my breath and ride it out. I'd die fighting the current if that's how it was going to be.

Then it occurred to me that this wasn't anything as grand as existential angst; this was middle age, pure and simple. Fallen-arches, potbellied, balding, gray, short-of-breath, irritable middle age. My father went through it and his father before him, and if you were a man of a certain type, you did everything you could to deny it. A mistress, a sports car, throwing yourself off a bridge half hoping the bungee cord will snap.

I began to hate Jayson, as if all this were his fault, somehow—Mirna, losing Mack, the various ideological shifts over the years, the loss of so much joy and faith and play. When all it was, was the natural course of things. The young came up. The old stepped aside, or were overthrown if necessary. We'd been doing it since the pilgrims, sort of like Trotsky's perpetual revolution, though here it looks more like *Death of a Salesman*. So I was not getting fired. I was stepping down, moving on to "pursue other interests," leaving my post to make way for ducklings like Jayson, whom the students will love. He'll be full of fire and enthusiasm until he makes it through his first review. Then depending upon how that goes, he'll start shaping himself toward some future tenure committee. He'll grow wary and look everywhere for how he's being perceived, who's with him and who's *agin* him. He'll develop little nervous ticks like unconsciously straightening his tie or a dry cough that shows up intermittently in the middle of his sentences. He'll begin to wonder why he ever came to Claybourne and if somehow he hasn't sold himself short and couldn't do better. He'll start sneaking looks at the *Chronicle of Higher Education* at the library—just to see what's out there. And he'll keep himself busy busy busy with committees, so he doesn't realize right off that an awful boredom has set in. He may take new drugs, start drinking in earnest, seduce a student or two. His work, though still energetic, will lose its edge. Even though he's determined not to, he'll start repeating himself.

Until he has days like today when he sits stupid and awash in self-pity, unable to look at his own work. Then what? Then you stand up and turn on the lamps and take a hard look at what you want to avoid. Or you squint. You sit and stare and think or have no thought … and then something comes to you. The painting speaks again, and you're there to listen, to respond, cautiously at first, and then more boldly. It's as if you'd had a falling out and were now making it up between you until the moment when each was free again to say whatever came to mind.

I may have moved too quickly, too soon, but I was desperate, so I began scraping away everything that was in the background, leaving Mrs. Montoya intact. But she wasn't intact. Her breast was missing, and the way I'd painted the scar still disturbed me. Was I exploiting her mastectomy for effect? But it was she who unbuttoned her blouse. And yet hadn't I been accused of creating a freak show in my work? Streetwalkers, the homeless, alongside portraits of poets and industrialists. And what exactly was I seeing in them? Or was I projecting something onto them, the way Catlin and Church made the Hudson River valley look like Bavaria or the first colonialists made American Indians look like Greek statuary, because the northern European could not yet see what lay before him, so alien was this new landscape and its people to his psyche.

Wasn't I doing the same thing? Did the world exist outside my seeing it? Of course it did. But in the end how would this portrait be distinct from my portraits of people back in New

York? Was my painting about anything other than what critics referred to as my style? Had I no vision? Was vision even possible anymore? An artist's statement, certainly, I'd written hundreds of them over the years. But that was more like a feint than anything else, a moment in the conversation that stopped further inquiry and allowed me to get back to the bar. It was a script I could refer to if anyone asked me what I was doing, because what I'm doing remains a mystery to me, a deep and private one. And so I don't talk about it, anymore than I would discuss my prayer life or my despair. Indeed I had no one with whom to talk about these things since Kate's death and Mack's desertion. I'd always been too proud or too stubborn or too private to have a spiritual director, and I feared all he'd offer was pop psychology or gimmicks to get me to start dating. In any case, he'd advise me to adopt a more conventional notion of God. But being a heretic is important to me. Being always a little at odds with God is essential. The uneasiness of the relationship keeps me awake.

14.

And keep me awake it did. All that night, I threw my body from one side of the daybed to the other—it was narrow, so one halfhearted flop did the trick. From time to time, I'd get up to drink a glass of bourbon and try to read. Maybe I was having a good old nervous breakdown. Just like me. Something retro.

I was weary and hungover—maybe still a little drunk—when Jayson arrived the following afternoon to sit for me. My back was turned when he knocked on the door.

"Come in," I said.

"Am I early?" he said.

"I don't think so. Sit down," I said, pointing to the chair.

I was a bit shaky, so I took another gulp of lukewarm coffee. Jayson seemed to be looking around for a moment before sitting down. I straightened my back and turned to look at him. He bounced his right leg up and down on the ball of his foot. He wore expensive sandals and new-looking black shorts with pleats in the front and a silk shirt with orchids on it.

"Stand up," I said.

He stood.

I circled him slowly and paused here and there to consider. He followed me with his eyes at first, then his head. I began to see where he carried his tension—his shoulders and neck. His hips and legs were steady. I began to focus.

I thought of painting the length of him, but so much would be legs, and though they were strong and brown and lean, it's not what I wanted. And yet I didn't exactly want him seated, either. He was too antsy for that, too hyper. I wanted to get something of that in the painting, without, of course, simply smearing his edges into a blur, for that's how he struck me— only here for a short time, hovering like a dragonfly, then off again. A profound restlessness, and yet I noticed in his eyes a capacity to focus his gaze intently, as if he could look straight through to something the rest of us couldn't see. His eyes were brown with amber flecks that shone suddenly in the light like mica, and they were now trained steadfastly on me, even as I was looking at him, yet not at him only, also around him, taking him all in, inside and out, placing, measuring, considering the dimension and size of the panel I'd use. Suddenly I saw him in three places at once. Three panels. A triptych.

There was a question in his gaze. I ignored it.

This was the longest I'd seen him go without talking. I liked him not talking.

"Walk around," I said, "slowly."

He moved self-consciously, swaying his arms in an exaggerated way.

"Slow it down even more," I said.

There, I thought. He'd settled into his body, his feet. He pulled his breath in more deeply. Still I had no idea what to do with him, where to place him in the studio, or where to begin.

"Take off your clothes," I said.

Jayson grinned and peeled off his shirt without unbuttoning it. He threw it onto the chair, kicked off his sandals and began unfastening his shorts.

Without his clothes, Jayson looked both more reasonably proportioned and more distorted—a gracefulness at odds with itself. Those long, long legs and bony feet. His arms were thin, his chest caved in a little, the sternum sunk, as if he were gathered around his heart. For the first time, I began to wonder about his history. I enjoyed the bow of his collarbone, and again admired his long neck and the way it rose to meet his jawbone.

I grabbed my pad, sat down, and began to draw.

"Relax," I said. "Don't pose."

This caught him off guard—he wasn't aware that he had been posing, and right away he let his shoulders drop and his face softened. Still I could see he was wary, frightened. He was so young, on the threshold of so much, and I viewed him with both pity and envy. For all his postmodern derring-do, he was still only twenty-eight and shacking up with a man twice his age who most likely bored and intimidated him.

"Good," I said, tearing off the top sheet. "Now turn. Stop. Turn back a little. Very good."

I must have drawn for forty minutes or so when I felt how

tight my own back and neck were, and I realized Jayson might be tired.

"Take a break," I said, pointing him to the kimono I had hanging on a post near the chair.

I put on the kettle.

"Coffee?" I said.

"No thanks."

I didn't encourage talking, and so we were silent for a while. I wondered what he was thinking, but I didn't want to find out, because if he started to talk, he'd chat instead. I liked the silence between us, and when he drew his breath in, as if to speak, I asked him not to.

Waiting for the kettle to boil, I closed my eyes, felt the edge of a migraine, breathed, felt it in the right side of my head toward the back. Still fuzzy from last night's drink, I thought, wishing I were clearer.

I stood up when I was ready to begin, and Jayson pulled off the kimono without a word and started walking slowly around the studio, looking at things—objects on the windowsill, plants, books.

"Jayson," I said.

He turned.

"Can you hold that?"

He nodded. He stood with his back to me, looking at me over his left shoulder, so that his trunk was twisted and there were two thin folds of flesh above one hip, and a smooth sweep of back rising from the other. I drew fast, the full length of him, from heel to buttocks, buttocks to shoulder, the tension in his neck, and then to the top of his head. The left side of his face was toward me, and in the eyes there was an expression I'd never seen in him before. What was it? Who cared? I just had to get it onto the page in charcoal. Something insistent in him, a kind of strength, a rootedness that went right down to his heel and the full surface of his foot, the way he stood there, or maybe it was what he stood for, something I doubt he could have ever put into words. It was in the viscera, unutterable, a pulse—beating. Whatever it was in his face had everything to do with the rhythm of his life, which was immediate, mercurial, always ready to flee. And now he stood, turned, looking back, called suddenly and unexpectedly, about to turn again and keep walking or take flight. That's why his right foot seemed so well rooted; it was about to propel him into the air. A sense of urgency, someplace to go, what his body knew that the rest of him—his résumé, his artist statement, his ambition—could never guess. It's right there in your body, my friend, I thought. Know that. Live that. Not the other. Not the galleries or the Biennials or Claybourne College.

I'd stopped breathing and the top of my right shoulder was in spasm. I took a deep breath and kept drawing because this way of seeing him might never come again. Then his face changed. What had been there was gone. Maybe I'd startled him, broken the spell with that sharp intake of breath. The moment had passed. It was over. I kept making marks, even as I said, "Okay. Move around." Somewhere in those drawings, I'd caught a glimpse of the painting, a triptych reading right to left, Jayson stepping from one panel to another, joining Henry in the middle (a portrait of Henry!), monkeys, magpies, and a bull snake uncoiling …

Then I dropped the pad on the floor, stood up abruptly, and said, "That's it."

In silence, Jayson put on his clothes and let himself out.

15.

The phone rang at eight twenty the next morning. It was Henry.

"Have you seen Jayson?"

"Not since he left here yesterday afternoon."

"What time?"

"Around three, I think, why?"

"He's gone. I don't know where he is. Could you come up to the house, Roger?"

That was the last thing I wanted to do. I'd awoken clearheaded from a full night's sleep without a hangover, and I wanted to get to work, but I said I'd be right there.

I found Henry at the dining-room table in his pajamas and a silk dressing gown, very Noël Coward, except that he looked terrible. He'd already poured me a cup of coffee. I sat down and waited for him to speak. In the meantime, I heaped sugar into my coffee and stirred, looking at a portrait I'd done of one of Henry's friends some years back. Something about the left side of the face still bothered me, felt unresolved, which at the time I'd thought made the right kind of tension. Today it seemed to me a lazy bit of avoidance and I remembered the moment I gave up on it. Then I began to wonder what had ever happened to Henry's friend.

"Where is he?" said Henry.

"That's just what I was wondering," I said and then realized we were talking about two different people. "You mean Jayson."

"Of course I mean Jayson. Who else would I mean?"

"Never mind. Where do you think he might be? Could you call anyone?"

"That's just it. No one I'd want to call."

"What do you mean?"

"There's a fellow who supplies us with recreational drugs—"

"Your dealer."

"I hate to think of him that way."

"So I guess the police are the last ones you want to call."

"That's right."

"Does he have any friends?"

"No. Not really. Not that I know of."

"A regular bar or coffee place?"

"I could try calling the Drama Club when it opens."

"Did you have a fight?"

"No. The last time I saw him, he was on his way to sit for you."

"Maybe it was something I said."

"What did you say?"

"Almost nothing. We spent the time in silence, mostly."

"How did you ever get him to shut up?"

"I pulled out my pad and charcoal and started drawing— works every time."

"I just figured he'd gone out. He does that sometimes. He hates for me to check up on him. We have an open relationship."

"And so he vanishes from time to time and then reappears?"

"Yes."

"Henry."

"What?"

"Aren't you getting a little old for this?"

"For what?"

"Drugs. Discos. *La Dolce Vita*. It doesn't seem to be making you happy. Wouldn't you rather settle down with somebody—"

"Oh, oh, oh," he moaned with his fists by the side of his head. "I keep trying. I thought I could with Jayson. And besides, who are you to talk?"

"But I'm different, Henry. I don't want to be in it at all. I'm too selfish, too caught up in work."

"There's nothing to do but wait."

"You can't sit here in your bathrobe all day."

"You're right. I have meetings. I'll go to the office. Roger, I'm"—his voice broke—"I'm scared."

"What can I do?"

"Go out and find Jayson and bring him home."

"What's your second choice?"

"There isn't one."

"Well then, you best shave and put some clothes on and get on with your day. I'll be in the studio."

"Roger?"

"And yes, call—if you need to. I mean it."

16.

I felt strangely elated when I got back to the studio and set right to work on the first panel, a full-length portrait of Jayson, as if once he'd disappeared, I could really start to see him. It seemed callous of me to be so excited about the new work, what with Henry's misery, but this is what I'd been waiting for—a way forward—so I plunged in.

I hung the gessoed hollow-core door on the wall and set to drawing the figure large, working from the sketches I'd made the day before. I worked fast and loose. The figure was turning—away and then back again. I sketched one figure right over another in soft charcoal until there was a real mess of lines that seemed to spiral down to the bottom right-hand section of the panel. It reminded me of the sense I'd had of Jayson being pulled in on himself. And it seemed to be that place that he sought to move from, so that the movement of the whole thing was toward the left edge of the panel. I thought of Mirna's theory about the yearning of two-dimensional objects, but this was a longing of another kind, who knew toward what, but within the same dimension, without destination, perhaps. Maybe the desire was for motion itself, velocity. The lines were at odds with themselves. They began to move with a kind of frenetic life of their own.

I sat and looked.

The phone rang. It was Mirna.

"I can't stop thinking about the young man you told me about the other day. And I haven't heard from him. How do I get a hold of him?"

"Good question."

"What do you mean?"

"Uh. I mean he's out of town."

"Visiting a college? Has he had a better offer?"

"Well you know, Mirna, he's a pretty hot property—a lot of people want this sort of candidate, not just Claybourne."

"That's why I want to talk to him as soon as possible. Get him up here early next fall—"

"While it's still presentable."

"—and have him see who we are, what we're about, our—"

"Vision. Mission. Values."

"That's right. Are you making fun of me, Roger?"

"Yes, I am. And I need to get back to work, dear. I'll tell Jayson you called. In the meantime, have a nice day, or an authentic day, or a deconstructed day, whichever you prefer."

And I hung up.

The whole time I'd been talking to Mirna, I'd been looking at the lines I'd made on the panel. I was just heading for the paint table to begin mixing my palette when the phone rang again. It was Henry from his office.

"Any sign of Jayson?"

"No," I said.

"Would you mind checking the house?"

"Yes," I said, "I would mind."

"I'm sorry, Roger."

"Look, Henry, my running up to the house to check on Jayson isn't going to make you feel any better. If he's not there, you'll still be worried sick, and if he's there, you'll be furious that he didn't call and you had to send me to find him."

"You're right. Listen, if you should happen to see him before I do, will you have him call me?"

"I will."

I hadn't taken two steps toward the paint table when the phone rang again.

"What is it?"

"Roger?"

"Yes."

"This is Jayson."

"Call Henry. He's at his office."

"I'm scared to. He'll be mad. I need your help."

"Since when am I the Department of Human Services? Call Henry. This is none of my business."

"I thought you were my friend."

"Jayson, I don't even know you. We have spent—what?— twenty-three hours together. If that."

"But I feel this resonance, this affinity. Could you lend me some money?"

"I'm sorry. You've dialed the wrong number. Let me transfer you to our loan department."

I hung up and then disconnected the phone.

I didn't feel like painting anymore, which irritated me to such an extent I didn't even want to study the drawing I'd done on the panel, so I turned back to Mrs. Montoya. The painting looked pretty bad, so I turned it upside down, which got my interest. I stared at it a long time, squaring off each section. It was too new to be fussing with it too much, but something told me I needed to pay particular attention to the architecture of this one from the very start. The window needed to be narrower, which is to say I needed to move closer in. The problem might have been the square panel, but then I began to see how I could make this work.

I grabbed another square panel and began to sketch out a new portrait in charcoal. If I put Mrs. Montoya there, closer to the window, just showing the edge of the sill with a band of bright light … that way I could stay where I was, not move in, keep the distance that was necessary to fill the picture plane and show the awkwardness of her position in the chair. I stopped and set the new panel next to the one I'd started and stood there squinting when I heard a tapping on the door.

"Go away!" I shouted.

"Roger?" It was Jayson.

"Call Henry. I'm busy."

"Roger, I kind of need to talk to you."

"Oh Christ," I said, and went to open the door. He didn't look good. His shorts were rumpled, one of the orchids on his shirt was torn open, and he had a black eye. As curious as I was—of course I was curious—I decided not to ask. "Call Henry."

"I can't."

I knew if I asked why, I'd be hooked, so I said, "Then don't. I'm working."

I started to close the door, but Jayson stopped me.

"I lost my key," he said.

I turned to grab the key to Henry's house off the hook beside the door and was about to hand it over to Jayson, when I thought better of the idea. If Jayson decided to rob Henry blind, and I'd let him in, I'd be an accessory to the crime. So I thought I'd walk him to the house. But then what? Would I stay and watch him? And if I let him use my phone, I'd be in on the whole thing, which I didn't want, so I thought of tossing him a quarter and telling him to call from the pay phone at Woolworth's on the plaza, but then I remembered that there was no Woolworth's on the plaza anymore. So I decided I'd walk Jayson through the garden, open the kitchen door for him, and then return to work. Being an accessory to grand larceny was preferable to losing a day of work, and I wanted to hold on to my key.

When Jayson tried to tell me what had happened, I held up my hand and said I didn't want to hear about it. "This is between you and Henry," I said.

"But I don't want you to think—"

"I don't think anything," I said. "Get cleaned up and call Henry. You two sort this thing out, and I'll get back to work."

"Thanks, Roger," he said, as I closed the kitchen door and headed back to the studio.

Though of course once I stood in front of the panels, I couldn't see anything for all the junk in my head. I kept wondering where Jayson had been and what he'd been doing and how he'd gotten roughed up. What if he were in real trouble, the kind that Henry feared? Well then what could I do? Call Henry? Not my responsibility. What if someone were after Jayson? None of my business. But what if it were a gang of cocaine banditos with semiautomatic weapons? I was really getting into the swing of things, and it was clear I wasn't going to do any more work today.

Nothing to do but lock up the studio and walk toward the Woolworth's that was no longer on the plaza.

17.

It's funny about Woolworth's. I remember the headline in the paper: WOOLWORTH'S CLOSES, GEORGIA O'KEEFFE MUSEUM OPENS—which speaks volumes about the way things have been going here in good old Santa Fe.

I loved that Woolworth's. I used to have breakfast there at least three times a week. The counter had its regulars, and though we didn't know one another well, we knew one another after a fashion. What I liked best, I think, is that I wasn't known as anyone but myself, a painter, no connection to Henry. And I ended up painting portraits of some of the people I ate with each week. I couldn't afford to pay them, so I'd do two or three canvases and let the sitter choose one they wanted to keep. Henry thought I was crazy to give away paintings to "those people," as he called them, who can't appreciate them. But I know they can and do appreciate the paintings. I've seen where they hang in their homes. They've shown me their own work. I have certain liberties being more or less foreign, and a traveler, not a tourist; an artist, not a developer. And because I keep coming back, people expect me to be here. "Ah, Roger," they used to say at Woolworth's. "Here you are. It must be summer now."

Toward the end, there was some talk about where we'd go once Woolworth's was defunct, but we couldn't really decide on anything. In fact, there was nowhere else to go in town that didn't feel like we were trying to be seen or even discovered by Hollywood talent scouts. So I got out of the rhythm of it, lost touch with the group, ate breakfast alone in my studio, and when I took a walk, felt more and more like a tourist.

Everybody talks about how much Santa Fe has changed in the last thirty years, and it's generally the people who've done the changing who have the loudest complaints. When I first started coming, people from the Pueblo would be seated on blankets and at tables in the plaza, selling jewelry. A few local crazy people would be roaming around, and some barefoot young people would be panhandling or playing music, mostly Anglo kids, refugees from some suburb back East or in California. Today they were all gone. Everyone was overdressed, except the Midwestern tourists in shorts that showed their knobby knees. The young people with backpacks looked as if they'd stepped out of an LL Bean catalog. In fact everyone looked like they were in a commercial, name brands showing on everything, as if they'd all been hired for a shoot, extras bused in from elsewhere, for one never saw the same person twice anymore.

Oscar Wilde was wrong. Life didn't imitate art; it imitated advertising, at least in this country. And Santa Fe had become just another theme park.

I was the oddball. Where could I go for a cup of coffee? Starbucks? Borders? Every place felt too much like being onstage, and yet I didn't want to face what awaited me in the studio, so I kept walking aimlessly, all around, until I stepped into the cathedral and sat with my eyes closed while a busload of Japanese tourists took photos, clicking and whirring.

I got up and walked along the river and through various parks, noticing how dry the grass and trees were. The drought was still intense, and people were being advised not to water their gardens, though the city had not yet started restricting water use. Suddenly a murder of crows appeared out of nowhere and began playing in a circle around me, squawking and swooping, as if they were laughing at me. And I thought of Kate, who used to feed the crows at her house every morning. At first they wouldn't take what she offered. I thought it was because she offered, and they liked to steal, so she'd pretend to be setting something out to cool, corn bread or a loaf of seven-grain or meat she'd just cooked, and sure enough, once she'd come back inside, the crows would descend and pick at whatever she'd left and return to a branch to see if they'd been caught. Then she'd storm out and shout and shake her fist at them. They seemed delighted. She'd go back inside, and they'd eat to their hearts' content. Gradually, the crows allowed themselves to be fed.

This offering was a ritual, one of many she lived by. Kate was a sort of pantheist, a pagan without the clutter. She made glyphs of cornmeal on the stones at her front door to honor the god of the day: Saturn, Mars, Mercury. Simple, to the point. She'd feed the river chocolate and wait for a favorite falcon to appear. She made an agreement with the deer: She'd feed them, if they let her garden alone. And it worked. I often marveled at the clarity and entirety of her faith. There was simply no question in her mind. Her relationship to the world was complete, even as it had its rhythms and variations. And yet there was nothing at all simpleminded about it, which surprised me. She was as tough, theologically speaking, as a Jesuit, and could argue you right back into the corner out of which you'd sprung. Like a magpie or a mountain lion or a bear protecting her cubs. Fierce, she was, and sure of herself, so it was a perplexing mystery how she ended the way she did.

18.

I didn't hear anything from Henry for the next few days except a phone message that said Jayson was back, so I figured they were kissing and making up, or working through it in whatever way they had of doing that. I tried not to think much about it, but kept remembering what Jayson said that night about making Henry mad and then sex being like fire. I kept hearing the vase break and their sharp, angry voices from the kitchen.

No matter how hard I worked, I seemed to make no progress. Sure I smeared paint onto panels each day, but I'd scrape off as much if not more than I put on. Mrs. Montoya continued to sit for me, and her portrait had come to resemble a bad Goya. It reflected none of her deep and abiding faith, and seemed to be a picture of my own increasingly distraught state of mind. She looked like Medusa or the hag who interrupts the feast at Camelot to give Percival a message. Not herself at all.

As for Jayson's portrait, well it was heading toward the pornographic. At one point, I'd turned him around and painted him with an enormous hard-on, like Priapus or Dionysius, perhaps. When he came back to sit for me, I turned him back around to his original position, and now he looked sort of like Lucifer at the urinal, casting a scornful gaze at an intruder—which would be me.

I couldn't sleep. When I did sleep, I had nightmares. I was drinking way too much. Evidently I was losing my mind, and so it should have been no real surprise that one day I found myself grappling with Jayson on the daybed, pulling off my clothes. After forty minutes of panting and churning around, Jayson said, "What are we going to tell Henry?"

"About what?" I said.

"About us," said Jayson.

"What about us? There is no us."

"What do you call this?" he said.

"This is not us," I said. "This is nothing."

"Oh I get it. 'Don't ask, don't tell.' "

"There's nothing to tell even if he asks," I said.

"Oh, you guys!"

"Who, you guys?"

"You and Henry and Clinton."

I had never before been compared to an American president, much less Bill Clinton, whom I admired and for whom I had voted. But this was clearly not a compliment.

"You're all hypocrites!" cried Jayson.

"Hypocrite is a strong word, Jayson. I think you'll find as you get older that life has certain unavoidable contradictions."

"Bullshit. That's crazy."

"What's crazy?" I said.

"This," he said.

"You're right," I said. "Let's get up."

"I don't mean that. I mean this."

"Look, Jayson. What counts here is Henry. He's one of my oldest"—I almost said only—"friends, and he mustn't be hurt, and that's all there is to it."

"What about me? Us? This?"

"I told you. There is no us. And this?—is clearly a mistake. I'm celibate, for chrissake."

"Oh yeah, right."

"Well, Jayson, that's one of those contradictions I was telling you about."

"One of the ones I'll understand when I get older."

"Exactly. Now look. It's not too late. We'll stop right here and now. Go back to where we were. You're the model. I'm the painter. You're Henry's partner. I'm Henry's friend. Just as we were."

"We can't undo what's happened."

"Well now, Jayson, I think we probably can—if we put our minds to it."

"I can't act as if nothing's happened."

"Of course you can. You're a performance artist, aren't you?"

"You're asking me to lie."

"Lie. Not lie. Let's look at it another way. We could … say … deconstruct what was, so that it isn't anymore."

"You're making fun of me," he said.

"A little," I said.

19.

The next evening, we were all at dinner in the big house with Henry's friends from Colorado, a retired couple looking for land—to retire from their retirement or for a vacation home, a getaway from doing nothing. One of them, Dan, a wiry, intense man about my age, had been a psychotherapist. I liked him more than his partner, a man in his sixties, plump and dull and superior, who was just plain rich and did what I imagine Henry did, which was to move money around and get richer. They'd been visiting Henry every summer for years, and now they were planning to move to Santa Fe. Henry was their real estate agent.

We hadn't even finished the melon soup, and already I was bored. Or anxious. I'm not sure which.

Dan was talking about his garden, the one he tended all summer long now that he had retired.

"The solutions are so simple, so direct," he said.

"It's not like you could've dusted your therapy clients for aphids," I said.

"No," he said, laughing. "Therapy was a lot harder."

"Do you ever miss it?" I wanted to ask if he ever felt bored or useless.

"Sometimes," he said. "Sometimes." And he left it at that.

He seemed to be intentionally not looking at his partner, and I remembered in previous summers, talking about our shared worries about retirement. I'd said I couldn't imagine it. Even if I stopped teaching, I'd still be painting. It was my life. How could I retire from my life? Besides, I'd said, I couldn't afford to. Dan had liked working with people, not just because it got him out of the house each day and gave him something to do but because he was genuinely engaged in the work. It had purpose. It made a difference in the world. I wondered if I'd feel the same uneasiness in ten months without a real job, at least a job that everyone recognized as valid. The impact of painting was intangible. Somebody bought it and hung it on a wall or put it in a closet or sold it in a yard sale. And how had I ever measured my effect as a teacher? A review committee every three years? Student evaluations? But what real difference had I made?

"So you're painting Jayson here," said Dan's partner.

"Pardon?" I hadn't been following the conversation.

"Henry says you're doing a portrait of Jayson. How's it going?"

I started to trace one of the gold veins in the marble tabletop with my finger.

"Going," I said. "Well. It's going well."

I looked at Dan and suddenly wanted to tell him how it was really going—horribly. How the painting looked more and more demonic and grotesque. How I'd ended up with Jayson on the daybed. How I'd betrayed Henry, our friendship, and my own integrity. That I was in spiritual crisis. "Help me for God's sake," I wanted to say, but I had a sneaking suspicion that I was beyond help.

I glanced at Jayson, who had a terrible look on his face: smug, self-satisfied—triumphant, really. I turned my attention back to the vein I was tracing in the marble. The conversation had stopped dead, and I felt responsible.

"And you," I said looking at Dan again, "what are your plans once you move to Santa Fe?"

I could tell this was an edgy question, even an aggressive one, considering his misgivings, but I didn't know what else to do. I couldn't stand being the focus of attention. Dan responded with something upbeat, chipper, if not a bit shrill, about his plans for an English garden here in the high desert.

Swell, I thought. What a great idea. And that's why people called us Anglos. We kept moving in crates of Wedgwood china and Waterford crystal, bottles of sherry and port—and English gardens. Never mind the drought. Just keep watering the primrose. And the vast landscape all around was nothing more than a backdrop and the Southwestern furniture, the blankets, the turquoise jewelry mere props in what remained an essentially European drama.

"So where are you looking?" I said. Real estate. Turn the talk back to real estate.

"Out around the opera," said Dan's partner.

Of course, I thought, where else?

"And I'd like to show you some places here in town," said Henry, "with more garden space than you'd imagine."

And so we ate. We sliced and scooped and chewed the wild rice and the lamb and the crisp fresh vegetables from the new natural-food chain store. We drank our wine and kept chatting. It is infernal, this chatting, I thought; it goes on and on. I was absent, not bored so much as preoccupied with the malfunction of my own mind, obsessing about Jayson, imagining I knew what he was thinking. He was enjoying himself, that much was clear.

"It's funny," he said, "sitting for a painter. It's like a seduction."

I could feel all the blood drain from my face. I took a good gulp of red wine. I could see that Henry looked curious and amused.

"In what way?" asked Dan's partner, though it was clear he couldn't have cared less.

"Well, first he lures you into his studio," said Jayson, looking straight at me and beckoning me slowly with his outstretched hand.

"Ha ha," they all said, looking at me.

"Then the sitter does a striptease—to please and ease the sleaze." Here Jayson stood up and started taking off his shirt.

"Ho ho ho," they all said, clapping their hands in a monstrous rhythm.

"And it's always the painter's version of reality that wins. He's the top man, the real daddy."

I coughed. The wine had gone down the wrong way. Dan's partner started to thump me on the back. I felt sure I was going to be sick. This was my punishment, the second circle of Dante's hell, and there I was among the lustful. I smiled, waving Dan's partner away, and tried to force a little "ha ha" of my own, but it was no good; I was dying. Not even Henry came to my rescue, nor did he seem to know that I'd been tossed forever upon the howling wind of everyone's derisive laughter.

Which is exactly what I deserved. For what is more ridiculous

than the self-deluded lust of a man in his middle years, especially
when he has assiduously avoided sexual contact for so long
out of some supposed dedication to something higher, to art,
who's nothing but an old whore anyway, who turns on you and
laughs when she's had her way with you—for I was beginning
to see the whole thing from a new perspective: the bottom of
a smoldering pit.

The talk turned away from me, and I sat vacuous, interject-
ing a halfhearted comment from time to time, just to let them
know I was still there, which I wasn't really. I'd left some time
before, in my mind walked through the little Japanese garden
and was back in the studio, contemplating the mess I'd made
on the panels and how it perfectly reflected the mess I was
making of my life.

20.

When Mrs. Montoya arrived for her sitting the following morning, I could tell by the look on her face that she wanted to ask
what was wrong, but she stopped herself and said nothing.
Not unusual. We often worked in silence, weaving our own
thoughts, perhaps sending them back and forth between us
without speaking.

The white scar, the window, the dark area to her right: I kept
working fast, all over the painting, from section to section. I
looked at Mrs. Montoya, then to the palette, and to the panel,
pausing for a moment with each shift, but only for a moment.
I'd caught something, or something had caught me, a current
in the river, and I had to let myself follow. I kept working like
this all morning, asking Mrs. Montoya from time to time if
she could keep going, and she said she could. We stopped a

few times for a short break, but mostly she sat, and I painted for nearly five hours.

And then with a sharp exhalation, I dropped my brush and said, "Let's stop."

It was as if we'd been riding the current together, no longer struggling, letting the river do the work, the way Mrs. Montoya had said she rode the rapids.

"You're not well, Roger," she said, buttoning her blouse. "You look tired. You work too hard."

I couldn't tell Mrs. Montoya what was going on. I was too humiliated. That I'd let myself fall to Earth, as it were, had betrayed one of my oldest friends and become embroiled in a sordid mess with a kid who took drugs.

"I'm not sleeping well," I said.

"Let me give you something," she said. "A tincture. I'll leave it by your door."

"Thanks," I said.

Mrs. Montoya turned to leave, then turned back. "Is there anything else, Roger? Anything troubling you?"

"No," I said. "It's the work. Another portrait I'm painting. I feel a bit lost is all."

"Ah," she said. "Now I know what to pray for. *Adios, hijo.*"

"*Adios.*"

21.

Her prayers must have worked, for I was left alone the rest of the day. The phone was silent. No one came to my door. I slept soundly for the first night in weeks and woke refreshed, as if the whole thing had passed: my obsession with Jayson, my betrayal of Henry. I had a cup of coffee before working up the nerve to look at the paintings.

First I assessed the work I'd done on Mrs. Montoya. I had to sit down. Her face shone clearly: calm and serene. The way I'd seen her. And yet the eyes said something else—not a warning, exactly, but a reminder. Stern and unequivocal, a plain statement of fact. The scar was the right color now and no longer looked like a punched-out crescent of bright white. And the way one hand rested in her lap while the other held her blouse open. It was nearly finished, and I was astonished. As if whatever madness I'd been in had burned away what was inessential and left something that felt true.

Then I turned to the allegory, as I'd come to think of it, the panel of Jayson changing direction. The face seemed less grotesque than it had some days ago. The expression was sharp, intent, clearly mischievous, but also beguilingly innocent. Still, some demonic energy shone through the body, torqued at an impossible angle, the strain showing in three different places. A monkey sat eating a nut in the right-hand bottom corner. And another swung back on a vine in the same direction as Jayson's gaze—toward the middle panel, the portrait of Henry, for of course it was Henry in the middle. Now I saw it.

I'd painted Henry a number of times before, always seated, always with his clothes on. The paintings had the feel of official portraits, the painter paying homage to the patron, like Max Beckmann's portraits of Morton D. May but stiffer, somehow, so that most of them ended up with various members of Henry's family in Texas; none of them had ever been exhibited.

Today I started with my charcoal freehand, from memory, or more from imagination, for it had been years, really, since I'd seen Henry naked. But I remembered the proportions, more or less, his belly, his strong thighs. I had him in an open-legged stance—solid, feet planted, knees slightly bent. Then I saw a breastplate, so I drew it, but how were his arms? At first I had them on his hips, like Superman (I suddenly saw the red cape flying out behind him). Didn't look right. What to do with his arms? Then I saw wings and drew them in a kind of fury. Wings. There he stood: an angel. But what kind of angel? Patron of the Arts. Defender of Good Taste. A sort of Daddy Warbucks with checkbook in one hand and Mont Blanc fountain pen in the other. I couldn't see it. How about the arms crossed over the chest? Superman again. Outstretched? No. He needed to be holding something, but what?

22.

The second part of the event began well enough with French cheeses, smoked salmon, melon balls, and prosciutto. Henry's annual garden party for five hundred of his closest friends. Not that they all show up at once. He invites them in shifts. The afternoon group is made up of Henry's straight professional friends: real estate clients, financial associates, bankers, stockbrokers. They're there from two to four and get punch and cookies, though it's a more elaborate spread—more like champagne punch and pastries from the Austrian bakery. Then from five to seven, it's a mixed crowd, straight and gay, financial and cultural. Henry breaks out the wine and spirits. The next group comes for supper from eight until whenever. It's a stag party, well, doe-ish with a few Bambis here and there, but anatomically speaking, it's entirely male, or that's what I would have said before Mack had made me aware of other options.

I showed up for the first group because a number of my collectors were going to be there, and this year more than ever,

I needed to remind them that I was still painting. I usually stay for most of the second group, but rarely stay for supper. Mostly it's that I get tired and am not, by nature, an extrovert. I'm only ever good for four hours of socializing before my eyes glaze over and I lose track of the conversation. I come away each year with frayed nerves and a whopping hangover the next morning, which costs me half a day of work, a sort of business expense, for if the collectors stop buying, there's no bourbon in the cupboard, no bacon in the larder, and no oil for the furnace.

But as I said, the second shift began well enough. As in years past, people chatted, admired the garden, talked about the drought, admired the house, talked about real estate prices, available properties, the stock market, the Biennial. Then the mood turned ugly. Someone knocked somebody else's hand and red wine splattered the small Agnes Martin painting. I was in another part of the house, and whatever the commotion was seemed to be over by the time I got to the dining room. It's not as though Henry has never had to have anything cleaned after one of his parties; it had more to do with who was responsible—a surly man in a black leather vest, no shirt—and it wasn't until much later that I began to put the story together. It was Jayson who'd invited the surly man without Henry's knowledge, and he'd come in the wrong shift. Most people in the first group had left along with the surly man, and the caterers were clearing up in preparation for dinner. I could see that Henry was furious, and Jayson was drunk. Henry stood pointing at the painting. I began to wonder what it would look like with more wine on it, how that would affect the broad white horizontal bands and the vertical drips behind. I imagined turning the painting upside down, but kept getting distracted by Henry's hissing. He was trying to lower his voice to keep the help from hearing.

His teeth were clenched, and I couldn't quite make out what he was saying. Jayson was positively stewed and swayed back and forth with a leer on his face. Then he said in a flat loud voice: "It's a $15,000 Venetian blind that doesn't even cover a fucking window!"

If there had ever in my life been a wrong moment to laugh, this was it, but I was so caught off guard, I couldn't help myself, knowing that this would most likely seal my doom.

Henry turned on me in a rage. Jayson went on swaying.

"YOU!" he said, pointing at me.

I stopped laughing.

"You're the worst of all."

And then I knew: His hand held a sword. Like the Archangel Michael. And I was so suddenly delighted to know this, it didn't seem to matter that he was about to lop my head off with it. I wanted to cheer, to applaud. I could see the barbarians at the gate. Throw them open, let them in. Fix them all a drink. Rape and plunder! Burn it all to the ground! Clear the land of art! Let's be done with it once and for all! I thought of Oliver Cromwell and his Puritan armies smashing the popish statues in King's College Chapel, and felt the kind of thrill they must have felt swinging the hammer to and fro. Which was odd because what I most wanted to do just then was make a new painting.

For there he stood, Henry, like an advancing general, magnificent in his full fury, sword raised, calling his troops forward to vanquish Beelzebub himself (that would be Jayson) but first he had to eliminate those around him of questionable loyalty (that would be me). And so I stood, awaiting my fate, my martyrdom, if you will, but with a part of my mind turned toward Henry's portrait.

"I've been betrayed by you both. Laughing behind my back,

taking advantage of my hospitality, my house. Then you," he said, turning again on me, "get Jayson to apply for a job two thousand miles away, at a college you've done nothing but deride and complain about for years, but which you portray to Jayson as something akin to Shangri-la. Traitor! Why do you want to ruin the only real happiness I've ever known?"

I wondered for a moment and then realized he was talking about Jayson.

"And you're not even gay! You don't even want him!" cried Henry.

I had no way of knowing what my face looked like, but my best guess was that the closed-lip smile drawn tight over my teeth looked more like the kind of face you pull when you knock your ankle on something on your way to pee in the middle of the night—more like a wince.

"Why, Roger? Why?"

Knowing this was a bigger question than I was prepared to answer at the moment, I was about to suggest we talk this over sometime later, but then the doorbell rang—the next shift of Henry's garden-party guests—so I stepped aside and let Henry pass on his way to greet them.

"Hello," he boomed. "Hello. Come in. Come in."

Jayson appeared to be comatose, though still standing. I couldn't think of anything better to do than vanish, so I let myself out through the kitchen door, as the caterers were busy working and whispering in excited Spanish about what they'd just heard.

23.

Despite a mid-level hangover, I couldn't wait to get back to work on Henry's portrait the next morning, especially now that I'd seen the look of pure, sweet, wounded outrage on his face and the sword of righteous indignation in his hand.

I drew quickly, placing him on the panel, in a three-quarter view, facing out, at a curious angle to Jayson's advance (as it now seemed to me) from the other panel, as though Henry were focused on one enemy while another slipped in behind him. Oh, he was going to be magnificent, Henry was, in this painting: fiery, golden, muscular, a plate of armor on his chest, feathery wings outstretched, stepping out of a cloud shot through with sunbeams, maybe, or not a cloud, the red dirt of New Mexico behind him, black rock with veins of rose. And suddenly—there it was, the bull snake. I could see it curling its way up Henry's right thigh. (Who was that who had a snake coiling up his right thigh?) But Henry seemed untroubled, as if the snake were an ally, something he could use to root him more firmly to the earth, just as he was about to step forward to challenge some evil—and he was going to win, you were sure of it—even as the mischievous Jayson was about to scoot in behind him (seeking protection, forgiveness, maybe—it was possible).

The phone rang. I'd forgotten to unplug it. I looked at it for three rings, and then picked it up. It was Henry.

"Roger, I'm calling to apologize."

"I'm the one who should apologize, Henry. I shouldn't have laughed. I love that painting. I've always admired Agnes Martin, felt her to be a kind of soul mate. I don't know what got into me."

"But I shouldn't have lost my temper, shouldn't have spoken to you like that in front of Jayson and the caterers."

"Don't worry about it. Let's consider it done with."

"Roger. Is Jayson there?"

Jayson had told him about the other day.

"No," I said. "Why would he be?"

"He's sitting for you, isn't he?"

"Of course. That's right. But not today."

Jayson hadn't told him.

There was a long silence.

"Then he's gone again," said Henry.

"I'm sorry." I meant this as an appeal for forgiveness and an admission of guilt. Of course, only God knew that, and for the time being, that was sufficient. "No I mean it, Henry, I'm really sorry."

"I know you are, Roger. And there's nothing to be done but wait. If you hear from him, can you tell him to call me?"

"Of course," I said.

I felt real remorse when we hung up, but I was also heartened by the possibility that Henry knew nothing of my real betrayal, and so I might still get off scot-free. Except for this remorse. Who was it said the sin is the punishment? I turned back to the charcoal lines on the middle panel for a moment, and then stepped to my table to start mixing paints.

24.

I worked steadily and well for three days without interruption. I'd rise each morning at six, make a small breakfast and a pot of coffee, and be painting by seven. Then I'd break at about noon and walk toward the plaza to find lunch—but mostly just to walk. Then I'd come back to the studio around two and work until I stopped for the day, poured myself a glass of bourbon, and fixed a little supper. It was just after I'd eaten and was sipping my third glass of bourbon, looking at the two panels, the one of Jayson and the wider one of Henry, that the phone rang.

Since I hadn't heard it for three days, I answered right away.

"Is he there?" It was Henry's voice, tired and defeated.

"Jayson?" I said. "No. I haven't seen him since you called—days ago. Still missing?"

"Yes," Henry said flatly.

"Would you like some company?" I said.

"Yes," said Henry.

So I walked through the Japanese garden, which was full of primrose and lupines and found Henry at his usual grieving station at the dining-room table (he'd never been one to sit in the kitchen), wearing his usual grieving attire, a silk dressing gown. He looked bad, worse than I'd ever seen him: Noël Coward meets Dostoyevsky. I sat down and put my drink on the table.

"I see you already have one going," he said, pushing a Moroccan leather coaster toward me. He had made a pitcher of gin and tonic. It took me a minute to notice that he'd replaced the wine-stained Agnes Martin with a portrait I'd painted of Kate some eighteen months before she died. I was so startled, I jumped back in my seat.

"Where did you find that?"

"I took it out of storage while Agnes is being cleaned."

Her sudden presence took my breath away.

"Does it disturb you? I'm sorry, Roger. How thoughtless of me."

So that was it. Of all the paintings, he'd chosen this one because he wanted to hurt me.

"Not at all. It's just that it's been so long—since I've seen it."

Kate stared at me in earnest, as if challenging. That was her look, and it was there in the painting. She sat at a table, paintbrush in hand, easel at her side, a crow sitting on her shoulder. Her hair was down around her shoulders, the window behind her open to the woods. In many ways, she was the bravest woman I'd ever known. She used to lash herself to rocks on the coast of Scotland, so she could paint the ocean during storms. She had some huge wildness in her. She met everything head-on, everything. And yet there was at the same time something vulnerable, almost fragile in her, an open place like a break in the clouds that shone through to limitless sky, a place she could not close up, and so she was left a little too open, it seemed, defenseless in some way.

Sometime after she'd been diagnosed with ovarian cancer, she cut me out of her life—deliberately, without explanation. And six months later, she was found hanging from a rafter in her studio.

Henry watched me as I studied the painting. I saw what he was after. He wanted to know if I was capable of feeling what he was feeling now, if I'd ever cared about anyone enough to be devastated by loss.

"Jayson's leaving," he said.

"He has an interview at Claybourne?"

"Yes, and he won't be back."

"I'm sorry," I said. What I meant was I was sorry for the whole thing, that it hadn't worked out with Jayson, that Henry was suffering, that I'd had a hand in it all, sorry that a part of me was pleased to know Jayson was soon to be out of the picture, sorry that we were frightened and greedy and small-minded and hurt each other. "I guess there's nothing to be done."

"Isn't there?" said Henry.

"What do you mean?"

"I'd hate for Claybourne to hire someone who turned out to be a drug addict."

"What are you getting at?" I said.

"Don't you think you should warn them?"

"It's none of my business."

"You made it your business that he apply for the job."

"Henry, I merely suggested it."

"No, Roger, you practically engineered it."

"I was only trying to help."

"By putting two thousand miles between me and my boyfriend."

"He doesn't even have the job."

"That's not the point. You drove a wedge between us."

I could see what was coming—the accusation, the trial, and the sentence. I pictured myself in sackcloth, head shaved, hands tied behind my back. I was doomed. I could stand dignified like the Christian martyrs who'd gone before me, or I could try to wiggle my way out of it one last time.

"Horseshit," I said. "Jayson was disappearing on you long before I arrived on the scene. I have nothing to do with his running off."

"Don't you?"

My breath stopped a moment. Then I said, "No, I don't," which is what I believed—mostly.

"It seems to me you've wooed him away with the promise of a job at Claybourne, as if you were saving him from me."

"Henry, what are you talking about?"

"You've always felt superior to me, Roger. And you feel Jayson can do better than this."

"Now that's not true." I was pretty sure Jayson couldn't do much of anything.

"Jayson admires you. He looks up to you. You can influence him. Tell him I love him. Tell him he can have what he wants here—teach in the East, live here with me, work, not work. I want him with me. Tell him that, Roger. He'll listen to you."

"He doesn't listen to anyone, really. And that's not the point. I can't tell him who and how to love. You know that."

There was a noise in the entrance way, and Henry stood up. It was Jayson, of course, letting himself in, so I took the opportunity to slip out the back.

25.

My original plan for the third panel was to show Jayson on the other side of Henry, having slipped behind the archangel unnoticed and sprinting off to … someplace like Claybourne. But the more I looked at the two nearly completed panels, the more I began to see myself in the third, the one that would constitute the left panel of the triptych. I resisted the idea because, as I've said, I never show my self-portraits, and these paintings were for my retrospective in the spring and meant to generate at least enough cash to give me a false sense of security with which to begin my new life as a vagabond, a word my grandmother used because she didn't like the words "tramp" or "hobo," since she would offer these men meals when they appeared at her kitchen door during the Great Depression. I began to wonder what would happen if I started turning up at people's kitchen doors at mealtime, when I was interrupted by a knock. I wasn't expecting anyone, so I was surprised to see Mrs. Montoya standing there when I opened the door.

"I'm sorry I'm late," she said.

Late. I'd forgotten she was coming.

"No problem," I said. "I'm running a bit late myself."

I had pretty much determined I was finished with this painting, so these last few sittings were to check details and areas that still troubled me. She unbuttoned her blouse and settled into the pose. After a few minutes, she said, "I saw the doctor yesterday, Roger. The cancer is everywhere now, moving fast. Inoperable, they say. They say more chemo, more radiation. I say no. No more. Nothing."

"I'm sorry."

"Don't be," she said. "I'm not. Not that I want to die. Maybe I won't. Father Juan reminds me that *todo es posible con Dios*, so I pray to accept His will. And I'm free. Ever since I got sick, I think, do I want to clean the house or read a book? Sometimes I lie around in bed, and nobody asks me to do anything for them. My husband is suddenly not helpless. He can run the washing machine all by himself, take the clothes out, hang them on the line. So they wrinkle. Who cares? And maybe he doesn't cook so good. Maybe he calls out for pizza. You know what, Roger? I like pizza."

I was thinking about Kate as I touched up the lower left-hand corner. I wondered what she would have said to me in those weeks before she died. How had she experienced cancer, her treatments, facing death? And why hadn't she told me?

"I'm happy, Roger. Strange as that seems. And I want to spend the time I have left in this world doing what makes me happy. So this afternoon, we go to the rodeo. Sunday, we go to mass and then my daughter-in-law's house for a picnic. I paint. I carve a little, though I haven't the strength in my arm anymore for bultos. I have cancer. I'm probably going to die soon. My heart is full, and I'm happy."

I'd stopped painting and stood looking from her face on the picture to the face I saw before me as she talked. It was and wasn't there—the mystery and serenity. She looked out from the painting, facing the viewer head-on. I thought of that last portrait of Kate. There was no self-pity or pathos in either picture, and still they fell short, in the way that all paintings fell short, which is perhaps why Mack and Jayson had given it up altogether.

"I think we're done," I said.

When Mrs. Montoya had stood up and turned back from buttoning her blouse, I let her see the painting. We were both silent for a time, and then she said, "So that's how I'll be remembered."

"Is this how you want to be remembered?"

"Yes, of course, Roger. It's beautiful. Hard to look at, but a beautiful painting. I'm a mother, a grandmother, a woman with one breast missing. I'll be remembered as that. But I also want someone to remember the girl I was, the bride, the young mother. There was no one there to paint me back then. Oh Roger. I was so strong. You should have seen me. And I could fight …"

I thought of Kate again and whatever it was that made her give up fighting cancer. I couldn't help thinking I'd failed her somehow, failed to love her enough, had become part of a world she could no longer abide, unsatisfactory in every way, implicated in a crime, some terrible wounding. If that was even it. I'd never know. Her suicide was an enigma. It was the way she'd done it as much as anything else, and even though I wasn't the one to find her, the image still haunted me. Still as a plumb line is how I imagined her hanging. She'd been there a number of days. I tried to leave the face blank, but sometimes I woke up in a cold sweat with it suspended before me.

There was something uncharacteristically sloppy and grotesque about her suicide, yet simple and direct, which was her nature, full of unanswerable questions, like her paintings. Her landscapes disturbed people. That's probably why they didn't sell. They were too big and fierce. People want to be reassured by landscapes, reminded of home, solidity, but Kate managed to render the tumult behind the scenery we saw on picnics and outings. She so often painted the scene before her in blizzards or thunderstorms. She depicted the river's undercurrents and not the flowing surface—as one drowning might see it in the last moments of life: detritus, fish, algae, shoes, tires, swirling, sometimes rising, sometimes falling.

"Let me give this to you," I said.

"No. It's not how my family wants to see me. It belongs to the world. I have something for you," she said, reaching into her handbag.

It was a retablo, crudely etched and painted onto a rectangular block of wood, some kind of lizard and a moth, much less accurate than her work usually was.

"Thank you," I said.

"I carved it for you. It's like a child's drawing. It's like I'm training a new hand to carve, while the other one looks on helpless but tries to instruct, like a good teacher, encouraging, not scolding. It's you and me. The salamander and a butterfly."

26.

I had no intention of burning Henry's house down. It was a joke, and it went wrong. That's all. Besides, most of the damage was confined to the bedroom, and Henry has excellent insurance, but getting the story straight is almost impossible now with everyone's imagination running wild.

I got drunk. That was my first mistake. It impaired my judgment. I wasn't even feeling depressed. Quite happy, in fact. The new painting was going well. Jayson had returned to the fold and so the phone wasn't always ringing. God was in His heaven and all seemed to be right at *la casa de Don Henry*. I'd decided to start the day with a little nip of bourbon. I do that sometimes, sort of take the day off, and by noon I had this great idea: I'd play a joke on Henry and Jayson. In other words, I wasn't thinking clearly, and by the time I actually got around to buying the fireworks, I was shitfaced. To celebrate Jayson's birthday, they had gone to spend the weekend with Dan and his partner in Colorado and were due back late Sunday evening, so I let myself in the kitchen door and crept around to their bedroom, ready to shush the ghosts of Duzzy and La Belle, Henry's poodles who had long since departed this life. Once in the bedroom, I arranged a long string of firecrackers on the floor all around the walls and under the bed. My plan was to run the fuse out the window and light it once they were asleep—bang-bang-bang-bang-bang-bang-bang! Just like the Fourth of July, which had been sort of a dud because of the drought. It's true, there was technically a ban on all fireworks, but these weren't the kind that posed any real danger. Little Chinese firecrackers. Just for fun.

Even with the official ban, it didn't take me long to find a fireworks tent. True, it involved quite a hike out Cerrillos Road, but with sunblock and my straw hat, I felt well protected. Luckily there were a few bars open, so I could refresh myself with a beer on the way out and back. After I'd installed the firecrackers, I came back to the studio and took a nap. Passed out is more like it. I awoke toward midnight, with a thoroughly parched mouth. I drank a glass of water and then a glass of bourbon and crept through the garden toward the house. I made a tour. All the lights were off. The bedroom windows were dark, so I crawled around with my flashlight until I found the fuse, lit it, leaped back into the Zen garden, sat on a meditation bench, and waited for all hell to break loose.

Pop … pop, pop, pop … Bangitty bang pop-pop-pop-pop-pop …

I expected to see Henry and Jayson any minute, running out in their boxer shorts. No. Jayson would be buck naked and Henry would have grabbed his silk dressing gown. But the look on their faces—I could hardly wait. Then I heard shouting behind me and the sound of heavy boots on the gravel path. When I turned my flashlight in the direction of the noise, I found myself looking down the barrel of a shotgun.

"Hello," I said, trying to sound nonchalant. "Who's that?"

Someone shouted something in Spanish that I hoped meant: Don't shoot!

"Mrs. Montoya?" I said.

"Roger?" she said. "Are you all right?"

"Yes, of course," I said.

"We heard shots. We thought there were robbers," she said.

"Oh no," I said. "It's just a joke."

Mrs. Montoya's son cried out and pointed to flames coming out of Henry's bedroom window. Before I could make a move, the Montoyas pushed me aside and ran toward the house.

"Henry!" I shouted. "Jayson! They're in there!"

I was suddenly stone-cold sober. I followed the Montoyas with their rifles. By this time the fire engines and an ambulance had pulled up to the front door, and people had begun gathering in the street to see what was going on.

Oh my God, I thought, I've killed Henry and Jayson.

I stood, paralyzed by fear, while the youngest Montoya went in through the kitchen and started calling out for them. Just then I saw Henry and Jayson emerge from the corner of the house.

"They're okay," I hollered. "Tell him they're okay. Get out of the house."

Mrs. Montoya darted into the kitchen to get her son, and my breath stopped. Her son came around the corner of the house, and I realized Mrs. Montoya was in there alone.

When I ran toward the house, I tripped on something and fell flat on my face. So much for what would look to all the world as my last heroic act. I was still very drunk, and I started to cry. I sat up, my nose all bloodied, and called out for Mrs. Montoya. Henry sat down next to me and put his arm around my shoulders. Another of her sons led Mrs. Montoya around the side of the house, so she was safe.

Someone—was it Jayson?—handed me a cup of coffee, which I spilled immediately.

"Oh Henry," I sputtered, "I'm so sorry. It was all my fault."

"What are you talking about?"

"I only meant it as a joke."

"What?"

"The firecrackers."

"What firecrackers?"

"The ones I put in your bedroom. I wanted to make you laugh."

Here I leaned over and threw up all over him and everything else. And the next thing I remembered was coming to sometime the next day with a real crucifixion of a hangover.

27.

Someone was knocking at the door, and the phone was ringing.

"Go away!" I yelled, but my voice sounded thin and dry. "Go away," I said more to myself than to anyone else. I threw a pillow in the direction of the phone. I missed and it went on ringing.

The door opened, and Mrs. Montoya stepped into the studio.

"Roger," she said. "Sit up. Drink this. It will make you feel better."

"Only death will make me feel better." Then I remembered. "I'm sorry. I don't mean that."

"Never mind. Sit up. Drink this."

"I can't."

"Trust me. It will make you feel better."

"What is it?"

"An old family recipe for hangovers."

I sat up and drank the greenish liquid. It was tepid and sweet, but even so, it began to quench my enormous thirst.

"I'm so ashamed," I said. "Is the house okay?"

"The house is okay. Henry is okay and his young friend is okay."

"I only meant it as a joke."

"We all make mistakes."

Just then Henry strode in, carrying a thermos of coffee and a bag of pastries by the look of it. My stomach turned, and I lay back down, groaning. Mrs. Montoya rose and said she was just leaving. She waited for Henry to step aside and let her pass, and Henry stood there for just a moment too long before he thanked her for all she'd done the night before.

"*De nada*," she said, bowing slightly out of graciousness rather than any hint of subservience.

"How are you?" Henry said.

"Thoroughly humiliated, thanks."

"Don't be. Nobody got hurt."

"But your house, your things."

"All of it is insured."

"But none of it can be replaced."

"I'm beginning to think Jayson is right. I'm too hung up on objects. They come and go. They're not what matters."

"But you love them. They mean a great deal to you."

"Maybe too much. And of course I'm upset to lose them—especially your landscapes, the first ones I ever bought. However, what's important is that you're all right, and Jayson's all right. And it might have been a good joke, if—"

"I hadn't burned down the house."

"The house is fine. The bedroom sustained quite a bit of damage, but I was about to have it redone anyway. This way the insurance will pay for it."

"You have a firecracker clause?"

"That's what I want to talk to you about. My insurance agent is going to want to talk to everyone, and you're not to mention anything about fireworks. Our best guess is the little Zen fountain on the dresser short-circuited, and the fire began in the wall somehow."

"But won't the investigators find the remnants of paper and the fuse and gunpowder?"

"If so, we'll say we'd bought them for the Fourth of July but didn't set them off because of the drought."

"But that's not true."

"It's true enough for the insurance company."

I wondered what Jayson would have to say about all of this. Evidently he hadn't told Henry about our little fling after all, and I imagined he might see this as one of those contradictions I was telling him about.

"Henry?" I said. "Are you mad at me?"

"Yes. And also grateful."

"How so?"

"I'm not sure I can explain it. No one I know, not even Jayson, could think of a more harebrained, idiotic practical joke that was potentially dangerous to even himself—and then actually do it."

"I wasn't thinking straight."

"You never think straight. You don't know how. That's what's so maddening about you—and wonderful. You're like a child."

"I am not. I may be stupid and impractical and imbecilic and unreasonable, but I'm not a child, Henry. Stop patronizing me. You have to be everybody's daddy. It's obnoxious." At this point my head started throbbing again, and I fell back onto my pillow.

Henry looked hurt and was about to defend himself, when I said, "Oh God! I'm sorry. You've come out of your natural generosity, and here I go insulting you."

"Never mind, Roger. I always take what you say with a big grain of salt."

"And you remember that I'm full of shit."

"Always. Give me a call when you're feeling better."

"I will," I said.

And after he'd gone, I whispered "Thank you" again and again until I fell asleep.

28.

I woke up in the middle of the night. At the foot of my bed stood an enormous woman. She must've been twelve feet tall. At first I thought Our Lady of Guadalupe had come to make me a Catholic once and for all. But she wasn't dressed right. She wore a loose gown that shone white and lavender and gold— something from the 1930s—and I thought of Noël Coward again. Blond hair hung down around her shoulders, and on her head she wore a garland of flowers.

"Who are you?" I said.

"Venus," she said. "And you're in big trouble."

"Now what have I done?" I said.

"It's more what you haven't done," she said.

Nothing in John Calvin or the Scriptures or even the confessional poets had prepared me to meet the wrath of Venus. She sounded sort of like Mae West.

"What haven't I done?"

"You haven't worshipped at my temple," she said.

"Oh God," I said.

"Watch your language," said Venus.

"What do you want from me?" I said.

"Actually, I kind of liked you on your knees in front of—what's-his-name."

"Jayson? But I'm not in love with Jayson. Don't be ridiculous."

"For you, we'll begin with lust. At least I got your attention."

"You're impossible."

"So people are fond of saying."

"Look," I said, "I paint. That's how I worship beauty."

"You call this beauty?"

"Now hold on a minute," I said, getting out of bed and turning on the light. "Sure, they're harsh, these paintings, distorted, maybe even a little grotesque, but look at how this pale blue is against the creamy beige; it's delicious. And that mauve in the shadow, the range of color in the black there behind the chair. I never use it out of the tube. I always mix my own. And here in Henry's wings—the brushstrokes, those feathers. This is the work of a Master!"

Though her arms were still crossed under her breasts, I could see she was weakening.

"But the overall effect," she said.

"That's a sort of beauty too. There's a sensuality in how it comes together, and a poignancy. The visual tension between, say, the set of Jayson's shoulders and the angle of his hips."

"Double-talk," she said.

"I suppose you think Botticelli had the right idea."

"Watch your step, bucko—he was a great painter."

"I'm not saying he wasn't. It's just that's not the whole story. He didn't get any of your fierceness, your rage, your vengeance. You're capable of terrible things. And you're petty."

"I'm not petty. Vengeful, yes. Petty, never!"

"All right. But you're not soft-headed or sentimental, either."

"Correct."

"In this country, you've been reduced to a Barbie doll."

"Oh stop," she said, shuddering. "I hate those things. They're like corpses. They give me the creeps. But you changed the subject. We were talking about what you haven't done."

"What if I painted you?"

Here she looked a little unsure. "After Botticelli and the others, I don't think so. I'm sorry, Roger."

"All right. I'll go to restaurants and admire young lovers. I'll paint them."

"You're pathetic," she said.

"Thanks a lot. So you came here to insult me. Are you going to help me out or not?"

"You figure it out."

"I keep trying. Apparently I keep getting it all wrong."

"Apparently. Think harder, dear."

"You're not going to make me fall in love, are you?"

"Roger, I don't make anyone do anything. I simply provide the opportunity."

"Yeah, right. What about Cupid and Psyche?"

"That was different. I'm his mother."

"So my loving counts for nothing?"

"It counts for a lot. It's your smug arrogance I can't tolerate, the way you hole yourself up, remain aloof, and think yourself superior to everyone. The way you find Henry ridiculous."

"But Henry is ridiculous."

"Of course he is. That's the whole point."

"What do you mean that's the whole point?"

"Being rendered ridiculous in the presence of yours truly is, in fact, an honor. I don't make fools of just anyone, you know. I'm very choosy."

"And you chose to make Henry suffer over a hophead."

"I gave Henry an opportunity to risk everything for love."

"But what's the point?"

"Adventure. A leap into the unknown. Humility. Wisdom. A richer life."

"Couldn't I just become a Catholic? Maybe a Penitente or something."

"You'd still have nothing but contempt for the world."

"That's not so. Just because I don't know the world, doesn't mean I don't love it."

"Nonsense. I'm on to you Calvinists. You refuse to know the world because you think you're not of it. You believe you're above it all—superior to the work of your own Creator. Talk about hubris! It's as if you're at the seashore, afraid to get your feet wet, and you blame it on God. You think it's what God wants, and it's not. It's not what any of the gods want. We insist upon full participation. Dive in! Swim. Sink. Drown. Who knows? Just dive in!"

"You don't care."

"That's not true. Occasionally we take a personal interest. Neptune shows up. One of us sends a mermaid, a couple of dolphins. Zeus—never mind about Zeus. His help you don't want."

"So why have you come?"

"Harm reduction. You're making a real mess of things."

"I know. I know! I should never have let Jayson into my studio."

"That's not the mess I mean."

"The fire, then?"

"Oh no, I got a kick out of that."

"What then?"

"Your soul. The life of your desire."

I realized I didn't know the first thing about it. The world was not just a mystery to me; it was a place where I'd never really lived, somewhere I had never belonged.

"All right then, I give up. What do I do?"

Venus sighed and pointed to the paintings.

"You mean keep working?" I said. I thought again of the priest who told Anne Sexton to look for God in her typewriter.

"Exactly," she said.

"But I thought you meant that I should give it all up, settle down with someone."

"Marriage?" she said. "Not my department."

29.

Jayson and I stood in front of his finished portrait. I squinted at it. I had no real idea if it was any good. I was still in that half-dreamy state of suspended judgment. At first it was just his soft, dry lips I felt brushing my neck. I didn't do anything to stop him. I went on squinting. I put my hand up to cover part of the painting. There was one corner that still bothered me, but I guessed I could live with it. Jayson went on kissing my neck, more forcefully, his hands on my hips now. I kept thinking: I should put a stop to this. Then I thought: What about Venus? He started unzipping my coveralls. I exhaled and leaned back against him, slowly, as if I were lowering myself into unfamiliar water at a steep spot along the riverbank.

Jayson led me to the daybed and finished taking my clothes off. As if I were drunk, as if I were a child, exhausted after a long day's outing. And like an exhausted child, I surrendered and fell asleep in his arms.

I woke up with a start. Disoriented and afraid. I looked at Jayson.

"What's wrong?" he said.

"Everything," I said. "I'm ruining everything."

"No, you're not," he said.

"Henry's my friend. I burn down his house. Now I'm in bed with his boyfriend."

"So what's ruined? A bedroom. Furniture. Objects. Henry's probably happier than he's been in his life—at least that's what he tells me. I may get a teaching job in the fall. You've nearly finished four paintings. So what's ruined?"

"Maybe it's me. Maybe I'm ruined."

"You really don't get it, do you?"

"If I have to ask what, I guess I don't."

"Henry and I are partners. He can't possibly meet all my needs. And I can't meet all of his either. We fight. We make up. We're not always in perfect harmony. Nobody is."

That's what I didn't like about the whole setup—the little dramas, the power plays, the fights, the gossip, the messiness. I wanted to sidestep all that and live only the pure high moments of revelation in my work. I didn't have much use for my species, though I wanted someone to talk to once in a while and someone with whom to play squash. I no longer had any real friends. Something—suicide, ideology, ambition—had stolen them all from me. People now fell into two categories: student or subject. Well maybe there was a third: pain in the ass.

I looked at Jayson.

"When you look at me like that, it's like you're from another planet or something," he said.

I thought of Venus. But it was more likely Saturn—or Pluto.

30.

I turned my attention to the third panel of the triptych. I'd painted myself standing at the easel, facing out and to the left, as if I were working on Henry's portrait.

I noticed I was standing akimbo, my bad posture, and there was something odd about how I'd placed my feet that made the whole stance unstable, as if I were about to topple over, as if I hadn't a leg to stand on, which seemed to be the case. And yet there I was: a painter, standing as painters have always stood and depicted themselves, continuing to work, despite their better judgment and public opinion. If I'd been younger, I might have made myself look defiant. But I never had been, really. From the outset I had portrayed myself looking tenuous about the whole enterprise … or as if I were having trouble keeping a straight face.

But here I looked intent—something between flummoxed and maniacal—staring out at the world: at Henry, at Jayson, the bull snake, the monkeys, and the magpies. I'd painted myself wearing my stained coveralls, with my bad haircut, my sparse beard, my work boots, one at an odd angle to the other, the window in back of me. All of it was there, and there was something missing, something that wanted to come out of the dark background, a shadow made by the light from the window.

I sat down on my stool and glared at the panel, willing myself to see it. Times like this, I regretted having ever given up cigarettes. That was the way to look at an unfinished painting—through smoke.

I thought of walking to the plaza to buy a pack of cigarettes, but I didn't want to leave the studio. I couldn't abide being in my own skin, yet there I sat, staring.

I got up and began to move the brush over the surface of darkness, coaxing, then pulling what I saw starting to emerge: a large figure standing behind me, a woman who refused to show herself and yet whose presence was undeniable. Then she receded again into darkness.

I was seized by a pain so deep that I struggled to find my breath. I sat down and could make out the eyes and the beaks of crows that perched on the woman's shoulders and along her outstretched arms. In the woman's expression, there was a sense of earnest observation—insistent and disinterested.

It might have been Kate who stood behind me.

All I knew is that I was painting.

Committing yet another heresy.

A necessary one.

We'll Meet Again

ONLY ONCE IN her adult life had Sally been sick to her stomach, and that was when she'd been pregnant with Melissa. She'd thrown up that once, and then never again. But now she felt a similar kind of stirring in her belly, which, because it was so unfamiliar, she first thought was grief, and then she knew: It was nausea.

Sally turned again to check if she'd seen right the first time. She had. The men were wheeling her father's casket into the church feetfirst. She cast her mind back to every funeral she had ever attended and tried to remember differently, but she was sure it was wrong. The coffin was supposed to come in headfirst. And it mattered. It must make a difference, even in a Unitarian church. She straightened her spine and took a deep breath to calm her stomach.

To Sally's left sat her daughter, a ten-year-old in braids, who wore a determinedly placid look on her face. Melissa swung her legs slowly, making sure not to graze the floor with her black patent-leather shoes. Between Melissa and Sally were two empty spaces reserved for her husband, Courtney, and her brother, Matt, who were pallbearers.

Across the nave from Sally, five large elderly women huddled around her father's second wife, Ruby, who was, as usual, making a lot of noise. A woman on either side of Ruby clutched her in their arms as she sobbed. Two more turned with handfuls of tissue from the pew in front, and one leaned over from the pew behind. Ruby moaned, she cried out, and when she had emptied her lungs of breath, she gasped for more, coughing and sputtering, then blew her nose for a long, long time. Sally wondered how a body could have that much mucus in it. She tried not to look over at Ruby, for when she did it only made things worse: up rose another lamentation, more piercing than the last. So Sally squared her shoulders, noticed her stomach had calmed, and looked at the podium where the minister, a man younger than she, would stand in a little while and deliver her father's eulogy.

The absence of a cross, the absence of an altar bothered her. In fact, were it not for her father's memorial flowers, the front part of the church would have been bare. From the ceiling hung an immense tapestry in which Sally was pretty sure she could recognize a fish, a candle flame, and the face of Thomas Jefferson, or was it William Greenleaf Eliot? As part of his eulogy, the minister was going to read a poem by Emerson and then, as he put it, "Open up the mic to anyone." For a moment Sally thought he was going to say "in the studio audience." He had asked her if she wanted to read something or speak, and she had shaken her head vigorously, though now that she thought of it, she'd have liked to read from "The Order for the Burial of the Dead" from *The Book of Common Prayer*—the 1928 edition—but she felt if anyone should do it, it should be a clergyman, and the Unitarians didn't seem to hold any more stock in the clergy than they did in the Liturgy, the Sacraments, or Other Rites and Ceremonies of the Church. To Sally's mind, the Unitarian Universalist church was nothing more than a debate society, a free-for-all with open microphones, and theology was something you made up as you went along.

Sally was an Episcopalian. She had become one when she married. At first, her father had been against it. He said Episcopalians were too close to Rome. But he'd been a good sport. During the months of the Great Debate, as it came to be called, he had accompanied Sally and Court to church on Sundays. He had stood when the parish stood, though he refused to kneel, and of course he didn't take Communion. It was the Lord's Prayer that made Sally clench her jaw. Her father insisted upon saying it the way he'd been taught and sang out, "debts as we forgive our debtors," while the rest said, "trespasses, as we forgive those who trespass against us," which meant her father always came out ahead. He went right along to the end without waiting for the others to catch up. Then he'd stand with his hands clasped loosely below his belt and smile.

Another wail rose from across the nave and Sally knew her father's casket must be approaching. She stood to wait for it to pass. The persistent little squeak of one of the gurney's wheels made Sally turn her head, and it occurred to her that she was the only one standing. Then she saw Matt's face, his eyes full of tears, trying not to laugh. She faced forward again until they had finished setting the coffin on the bier and bent to smooth her skirt before sitting down again. She was sure one stood for the casket when it passed. Then she wasn't sure at all. Was that for weddings? One stood for the bride. At any rate, it showed respect. She'd been taught to stand when an adult entered the room, and her father, though dead, was still an adult.

Which was more than she could say for her younger brother, who had chosen not to wear a dark suit and a white shirt and black shoes. Oh, no. Not Matt. There he was at his own father's funeral in a blue seersucker suit, a jaunty boutonniere in his

lapel, and white bucks. All he needed was a boater and a uku-
lele. It was just the sort of thing their father would have been
wearing, had Sally not insisted he be buried in his charcoal gray
Brooks Brothers.

The older Matt got—he was now thirty-five or thirty-six—the
more he looked like their father: solid, broad, with thick dark
hair and light eyes, the exact same cleft in his chin. And they
had similar natures—exuberant, expansive, outrageous. They
were always trying to outdo each other in childish, stupid ways
with a joke or a wild tie. They'd fight, not speak, then make up
and become inseparable again. They adored each other. Sally
felt it was quite unnatural. Just then Matt caught her gaze and
winked. She glared back at him until he looked away.

Before coming back into Sally's pew, Matt stopped to comfort
Ruby, who struggled to her feet, made it past the clutching
women so she could hang on him. Matt had pretended to like
Ruby from the very first because he always sided with their
father against Sally, and because he was trying to prove how
open-minded and accepting and contemporary he was. Oh,
it was all fine for him: He lived in Santa Fe, owned a gallery,
palled around with the jet set, got married every two weeks.
But if he had come back to St. Louis, married some nice girl
from a good family, gone into a respectable business … If he'd
only gone to Vanderbilt instead of Reed College … Or if their
mother hadn't died.

By now Matt had installed himself between Courtney and
Melissa and they were all waiting for the minister to begin. Their
father was a good man, he said. He was a family man, a fair
man, a man who distinguished himself in the business world,
a man who served his community. Sally couldn't stop thinking
about Ruby's dress. It irked her. True, it was black, she was

thankful for that, but it was a rustling, chiffony thing, more of a cocktail dress, with a neckline that was just low enough to be inappropriate. And the veil was attached to this funny little pillbox hat of black satin that looked like something a bellhop would wear. It hung way over her face, past her shoulders, and ended in a thick black ribbon. It had tiny red-felt polka dots all over it, which, up close, turned out to be hearts. In her enthusiasm for grieving, Ruby had not always managed to get the tissue under the veil before she blew her nose.

Her father had met Ruby at a bowling alley. They had ended up on the same team. His physician had suggested he get more exercise. Why hadn't he chosen tennis or squash, something the other men played? And he had a perfectly good membership to the country club where he could have played golf; but no, he had picked bowling. And that's where he had met his second wife. His widow. The woman who sat blubbering in the arms of badly dressed women across the nave.

Sally remembered a visit she had made to her father's house shortly after he started seeing Ruby. When she came up the long driveway she noticed a man holding a tall canister with a slender rubber hose, spraying the box hedge. She hadn't thought a thing about it until she noticed that the part of the hedge he was spraying was a different color than the rest. Even before she kissed her father inside the front door, she asked what was wrong with the hedge.

"Nothing," said her father. "It's just the wrong color."

"But it's always been that color."

"I know. What better reason to change it? Besides, it clashes with Miss Ruby Lubeck's car."

"You mean that man out there isn't spraying for bugs? He's—"

"That's right. He's painting the hedge."

"But you can't."

"I know I can't. That's why I hired him."

"That's not what I mean. I mean that was Mother's pride, that hedge. Don't you remember? She loved it and now you're going to kill it. The leaves can't breathe with paint on them."

"Settle down. It's more like a tint. The hedge'll survive. Want some coffee?"

Sally was too confused for coffee. She wanted to call someone, to have him stopped, but this was his house; she had no legal right. Just then, Ruby rounded the corner from the dining room, carrying a silver tray with coffee cups and sweet rolls.

"Well, hello there," she said. "Won't you join us for a little coffee break?"

Sally wondered what this woman was doing serving coffee in her father's house this early on a Saturday morning.

"No, I won't, thanks," said Sally. "I mean, I can't. I have to be on my way. I just came by to …" Her mind went blank. What could she possibly have come here to do? Visit with her father. Alone. And here was some jackass painting her mother's box hedge a lighter color of green so it wouldn't clash with the car of this … woman, her father's— And it was this horrible, cheap color, a kind of limy green with too much yellow in it that hurt to look at. "I just dropped by to"—Sally looked around the room in a panic; she didn't know what to do with her hands—"to see if you might still have Mother's old tennis racket. I've broken a string on mine and thought I'd use hers if it's around. But come to think of it, I have it somewhere at home. Isn't that silly of me? I must be getting absentminded. I drive all the way over here and …" Sally looked out a dining-room window just in time to see the man in coveralls pass by, followed by a solid block of the limy green that made her want to tear at her hair. Or that woman's. She smiled at Ruby, kissed her father on the cheek, and made her way to her car in several small, deliberate steps, grinding the white driveway gravel under the soles of her flat shoes.

The first thing she did when she got home was call Matt. He laughed. He just sat there on the other end of the line and laughed his fool head off. "That's great," he kept saying.

"No," said Sally. "It's not great. I don't see anything the least bit great about it. And it's not just the hedge, Matt. It's the whole situation. The way he's been acting. This woman."

"That's your real beef, his new girlfriend."

"Matthew, don't call her that. She's not Daddy's new girlfriend, not his girlfriend at all. No such thing."

"What have you got against her?"

"Well, she's so, I don't know. Loud."

"So's Dad. They probably get along fine."

"That's not what I'm worried about. Did you know they met in a bowling alley?"

"Yes, so what?"

"She's just not our sort of person, that's what."

"And what sort of person is that?"

"Oh, you know what I mean."

"Not black, not Chinese, not Catholic."

"Matt."

"Not blind, not crippled, not hunchback."

"Oh, shut up, Matthew! Please. I am trying to discuss our father. This is a long-distance call. I am paying. Now quit. What I'm trying to say is: I am afraid something might have affected his mind. Do you suppose he could have had a small stroke?"

"Sally, has it ever occurred to you that Dad might be happier than he has been in years? Let him do what he wants. His life is none of our business. Just butt out."

"I should have known better than to turn to you for help. You've been shirking every single family responsibility since you were eight."

"Since when is interfering in my father's sex life a family responsibility?"

"This has nothing to do with sex. You simply won't see. You never have. Not you. Off you went into the Great Northwest to smoke marijuana. Then you saunter down to Santa Fe, make a fortune off trendy painters, go around wearing turquoise jewelry and cowboy boots. Yippee-i-o-ki-ay! But who's left to do all the worrying about what everyone's going to think when our poor father goes insane? Me! Always me. You've never given me any help in this. You've never even given Daddy any grandchildren."

"Hold on, Sally. If this is the full version, I'll have to get off the phone. I'm due at the gallery at one."

"Benedict Arnold!"

"Oh, stop, for chrissake. There's nothing to worry *about*. Leave the poor man alone. If Dad wants to spend time with the woman he loves—"

"He cannot possibly. She is just too—"

"—the woman he *loves*, he's perfectly free to do so. He's a grown man. Eccentric habits or no, he's all grown up and he deserves to have his own life just as much as you or I do."

Of course Matt sided with his father. He thought it was marvelous. He thought it was grand. Their father was having the time of his life parading this … *woman* around in public. Men only ever thought of themselves. Or each other. Which was just another way of thinking about themselves. She was grateful for Courtney who was different and whom she now touched with her elbow because he had relaxed his jaw and was breathing through his mouth, which made a disagreeable snoring sound, so he closed his mouth and breathed through his nose. Every once in a while she had to remind him.

The minister began reading the Emerson poem:
"Give all to love;
Obey thy heart;
Friends, kindred, days,
Estate, good-fame,
Plans, credit and the Muse,—
Nothing refuse."

Her father had certainly refused Ruby nothing. Sally suspected he had left the bulk of his estate to his new wife—they hadn't yet celebrated their second wedding anniversary. She didn't mind so much. She had long ago received her share of her mother's wealth, and Courtney was a successful lawyer. He'd seen earlier than most the profitable future of bankruptcy. He litigated, he liquidated, he made money hand over fist. Matt and her father referred to Court as "the Vulture," just between themselves, but she knew it, and, unfortunately, Courtney had a large beaklike nose and a bald spot on the top of his head. Her father had found him bland, dispassionate. He complained he never could get a handle on what Court thought or how he felt about a matter. To Sally, her husband was a welcome relief. He was quiet and stable. He lacked the gush and thunder of the men in her family.

No, it was not the money Ruby would inherit that bothered Sally; it was the principle. Sally's shoulders began to shake a little and she lowered her head to laugh quietly at her own joke. Of course it was the *principal*. Courtney put his arm around her; evidently he thought she was weeping. Sally coughed, waved him away with her handkerchief, and sat up straight again.

The minister called Matt to the microphone. When Matt got there, he took a sheaf of papers out of the inside pocket of his jacket, smoothed the pages onto the podium, and said he was going to read his father's favorite story, "The Celebrated Jumping Frog of Calaveras County." Sally closed her eyes and went limp against her husband.

Ruby let out a little squeal of delight, and wiggled back and forth. She gave her nose a short honk and hushed her chorus of female mourners. Patting one on the shoulder, she said, "Do you know this one, Shirley? It's by Mr. Mark Twain. Oh, I love it. I really do. Now shut up everybody and listen."

Sally could feel a slow, even throb starting in the back of her skull. She had to pick up the mourning cards at the engraver. Those close to the family, she could write to on her own stationery. She began to categorize by importance: size of the flower arrangement, length of association with Daddy's business, old friends of her mother's. She had this to do, and now this headache—what better excuse to avoid gathering with Ruby and the others at her father's house after the service.

"Well, thish-yer Smiley had rat-terriers, and chicken cocks, and tom-cats and all them kind of things, till you couldn't rest, and you couldn't fetch nothing for him to bet on but he'd match you," read Matthew. Oh, it was all so phony, this down-home nonsense. Her father had gone to Dartmouth, for heaven's sake. His love of tall tales and backwoods folklore was an affectation.

And yet, that must have been what attracted him to Ruby. Larger than life, rawer than one would think possible, it's as if she had stepped out of a frontier tale. She had grown up out West, in Tacoma, Washington, for the most part, though she and her mother had traveled a good bit. Her mother was "on the stage," as Ruby put it. They lived in hotels, which, for some reason or other, kept catching fire. So she remembered her childhood as a series of late-night escapes from burning buildings, with people "hollerin' and cussin' and brawlin' " all around her. This she recounted to Sally in the middle of tea at the newly opened Ritz-Carlton. Sally had invited her as a goodwill gesture when Ruby and her father became engaged.

Ruby had worn a midnight-purple dress with enormous, glaring white gardenias printed all over it. She was just that much too enthusiastic about every little detail. "Oh! Isn't this lovely! Just look at these drapes! And this carpet! My!" Clearly Ruby felt out of place. But Ruby's discomfort didn't seem to last long. Soon enough she was telling the story of her life: "You know, my mother was really a stripper. Not that there's anything wrong with it—the human body is beautiful, a work of art, really. But I wanted to sing and be a *real* dancer. I vowed to myself to keep as many of my clothes on as I could. Well—in the end, I was singing lonely hearts cowboy songs in a piano bar in Beaumont, Texas. That's where I hit bottom. But shoot, my bottom got hit so many times, it was already black and blue." And then she laughed, this horrid, high-pitched, yahoo cackle.

"You never see a frog so modest and straightfor'ard as he was, for all he was so gifted," Matthew read on. And on.

By the time he finished, Sally had organized her procedure for answering sympathy cards and decided which pieces of furniture to get rid of to make room for what she felt sure was coming to her from her father's house. She wondered if Ruby might not decide to stay in the house after all, though she had always been trying to get her new husband to move "out of this big old house" to "one of those cute little condos" near the Neiman Marcus mall.

The minister nodded to Ruby, who stood up, flipped her long

veil back over the top of her head, stuck a hankie in her sleeve, and made her way to the podium. She stood for a moment, looking out at the people in pews. Her face seized up in a grimace, and she began to cry again. Sally looked down and pulled the ring finger of her left glove. She jumped when she heard Ruby blow her nose—right into the microphone.

"I'm going to sing a song," she said.

Perfect! thought Sally. Why not? We've had everything but performing dogs at this funeral.

"A song that meant a lot to our generation. A song our whole bowling team sort of adopted. A song Jack and I loved."

Sally had forgotten to breathe, and her sudden, sharp intake of air made her husband turn to see what was the matter. He reached for her hand. She snatched it way. She was white with rage.

"*We'll meet again. Don't know where. Don't know when. But I know we'll meet again some sunny day.*"

Sally heard people moving around behind her, way in the back. Probably leaving, she thought.

"*Keep smilin' through. Just like you. Always do. Till the blue skies drive the dark clouds far away.*"

It sounded more like a commotion than just a few people getting up to leave, so Sally turned around.

People were dancing! One by one, the older folks were getting up out of the pews and choosing partners. They started to fill the back of the church and make their way up the nave and into the aisles. Smiling. Some of them were chuckling. All these people from her father's bowling team, for who else could they be? But then she recognized some of her family's oldest friends—from before. They were all standing up to dance at her father's funeral. It was as if demons had sprung out of the floor to mock her.

She yanked herself around to face the front, and there was Ruby, still wailing away: "*They'll be happy to know. That as you saw me go. I was singing this song. We'll meet again.*" When Ruby opened her eyes and saw everyone dancing, she smiled and went on with a new power in her voice. "*Don't know where. Don't know when.*"

Sally took a deep breath. She had gone along with everything so far: a free-form Unitarian service, an open mic—even Matt reading "The Celebrated Jumping Frog," she could endure. But this. This was—she stood up and sat back down again. Courtney looked over at her with a soft, sympathetic expression. You, she thought. Why don't you do something? But he wouldn't. He never did.

"*Keep smilin' through. Just like you. Always do.*"

Sally tied two fingers of her glove together and pulled tight. Matt stood up. For a moment Sally thought he was going to do something to stop all this, but when he headed for the back of the church, she realized he'd gone off to find a partner. The women on Ruby's side of the church danced with one another, and those not dancing swayed back and forth, humming along. Then Sally's daughter, the child formed out of her own body, who took after her in every way possible, tugged at Courtney's sleeve and said, "Can I dance, too, Daddy? Can I?"

And Ruby went right on singing. When she finished a verse, she started over again at the beginning, her voice growing clearer, richer, younger. Sally wanted to put her hands around Ruby's throat and press her thumbs into the soft flesh to choke off her air. Courtney put his arm around her and whispered, "What do you say? Shall we join them?" Sally didn't turn her head. She was afraid that if she looked into those warm brown eyes of his, she'd claw them from their sockets. Courtney and Melissa slid out the other end of the pew to join the dancers. Sally glared at Ruby, who rocked this way and that, leaning into a favorite phrase, her eyes closed, pleased with herself, Sally supposed, that she had managed to disrupt the whole funeral, draw everyone's attention away from the corpse and hog it all for herself.

It wasn't fair. Ruby had buried three of her five husbands, and she might well live to bury a fourth. She would have all kinds of different funerals to attend. But Sally had only one father, this was his only funeral, and his stupid second wife had gone and ruined everything. Or her father had—by marrying Ruby. Someone was to blame. And just as Sally raised her eyes to the tapestry that was hanging behind Ruby, she thought: Maybe it was Thomas Jefferson—or *was* it William Greenleaf Eliot? All Sally knew was that everything had been ruined.

Struggling into her coat, she stood up, grabbed her pocketbook and gloves, and turned to leave, but there was no path between the dancers. She began to shoulder her way through the crowd to the back of the church. They reached out to touch her, to clasp her hand. They smiled, and at first, she smiled back automatically. Then she looked straight ahead and pushed harder. When hands came at her, she batted them away. She punched shoulders and shoved people off. She dropped her gloves, but kept on driving through toward the door.

When Matt appeared and threw his arms around her, she fought to free herself. She pushed and squirmed and grunted. "Let me go," she said. "Matthew! Let me—" But he held her and held her, stood firm and went on holding her until for some reason the fight drained out of her body. And as Matt moved her gently, with perfect assurance, into a slow graceful fox-trot, Sally put her head down on his shoulder and began to sob.

A Wedding Song for Poorer People

1.

T<small>HE TRAIN HAD</small> been stopped a long time in the middle of nowhere.

"Not nowhere," said Yuri. "This is Russia."

"But why here? There's no station," said Irene.

Yuri set down his glass of tea. He shrugged.

"Arthur," she said, "go find out what's happening."

Arthur looked at Yuri, whom he was beginning to like a great deal, looked back at Irene, and then shrugged. Irene turned to Molly for support, but Molly kept her gaze fixed on something outside the window.

They waited. For hours they waited into the night, without explanation, in what Yuri called Russia, but what Irene still thought of as nowhere.

"Do you suppose we've broken down?" she said, more to herself than to anyone else. "Must have. Can't be a frontier; there'd have been customs officers."

Arthur sat next to Irene. He kept looking up from his book to gaze at Yuri, their guide, a short, square-shouldered man of about thirty, with a broad face and a head full of white hair.

135

Premature, thought Arthur, who had passed fifty and whose own ash-blond hair was growing quite thin on top. He returned his glance to the book on his lap for fear of being caught staring.

Yuri picked cherries out of a paper sack, one after another, and tongued the pits into his palm, lowering them into a square of newspaper he'd fashioned into a cone. He turned to offer the cherries to Molly.

"No thanks," she said without smiling.

Molly was a small, powerfully built woman in her late thirties. A good athlete in high school and college, she'd kept in shape these last fifteen years by doing everything in the theater except walking onstage to play a role. Her genius was for life behind the scenes, which is why she was not only directing the play but also served as production and company manager.

Molly could see that Arthur was falling in love with Yuri. Old fool! She was furious. The tour had not gone well so far. Rather badly, in fact. Not enough rehearsal time and a misunderstanding about the musicians' contracts in Prague. In Warsaw some poor girl had set her heart on one of the actors, Burt, who swore up and down he'd done nothing to encourage her. "Just being friendly," he said, and yet there she was at the stage door each night, weeping and wailing, then pleading with them to give her a job, take her with them. "Anything," she said. She'd do anything at all.

Molly stared hard out the train window, trying to penetrate the dark. She remembered a train trip West with her mother to visit relatives years ago, the way space opened up once they were out of New England, this same sense of limitless land and sky, only here in Russia there were no lights anywhere, and rolling through Kansas in the middle of the night, she could always make out a lit window somewhere in the distance, or a

light pole where two roads crossed at the corner of a field. Here
there was nothing.

Molly thought of how, as a girl, she had stood for hours in a
clearing in the woods not far from her house in New Hampshire,
waiting for the Blessed Virgin Mary. Her devotion was fervent.
She was more ardent in her desire than the children at Lourdes,
she was sure, so it was only a matter of time until she would have
her vision. She would stand very still, barely breathing, as if the
Queen of Heaven were as skittish as a dragonfly. When Molly
reached a state near ecstasy, due to lack of oxygen more than
anything else, she'd return to her mother's kitchen. Although
social and active at school, she would enact this solitary ritual
of waiting two or three times a month, even in the dead of
winter. And because she so often felt transported, she was never
disappointed for want of an actual visitation.

Now, from the window of a stranded Russian train, she
thought she caught sight of movement outside in the mauve
shadow: smoke or mist propelled by some narrow current of
air. Something that looked like a silk scarf. Then light, as if
passing through a facet of amethyst or garnet, and rounding a
shape, a forehead, perhaps. Molly was sure she heard faint bells,
the kind sewn into the hem of a dress or worn on the ankle,
as if there were a wedding procession outside the train, people
sighing, murmuring, singing, as they stepped together, hands
clasped, turning to look into one another's eyes, turning their
gaze skyward, sure of their footing, though there was no moon
and the stars were covered by clouds.

2.

There was a knock on the door. Burt stuck his head into the

compartment.

"What's going on?" he said.

"We've broken down," said Irene. "We must have."

"What's the problem?"

Burt looked as if he were about to roll up his sleeves and repair the train himself. He was stout and bald, with thick forearms.

"They're not really sure; they're seeing to it," said Irene with tenuous authority. "Don't imagine we'll be much longer. Nothing to worry about."

"Let the others know," said Molly.

"Sure thing," said Burt, leaving.

Irene turned to Yuri.

"There is nothing to worry about. I mean, we needn't worry. I am correct in assuming this, am I not?"

Yuri sat back with his hands behind his head, feet outstretched and crossed at the ankles.

"Correct," he said, not bothering to open his eyes.

Irene sighed and something caught in her throat, making an exasperated little sound. She turned to the window, but all she could see was her own reflection and Yuri dozing and Arthur looking at Yuri and Molly with her head now bent toward the book on her lap and their jackets all hung on hooks to either side of the door and the tea glasses on the little folded-down table. She stood up and tried to lower the window, but it wouldn't budge. She turned toward the men, both of whom now had their eyes closed, and was about to ask Molly to help, when she thought, *bugger* it, and swept out into the corridor to smoke.

There she found a lowered window she could lean out. Beyond the squares of light from the railway carriages, there was nothing but dark, uninterrupted by even the suggestion of a tree, for there were no stars; it had been raining all over Eastern Europe since they'd begun their tour six weeks earlier in Prague. Then Warsaw. And now they were headed toward Leningrad. She had so looked forward to this, and now here she was: peevish and irritable. She'd have to make it up to Arthur, and it wasn't fair to poor Molly, whom she'd cajoled into coming. The tour had been a disappointment thus far. Irene had expected a better reception, more enthusiasm. What seemed such a good idea back in London now seemed quite ridiculous.

"You see," Hal said, "it's not a Marxist play anymore; it's about the new *entrepreneur* in Russia, in Eastern Europe. Mack the Knife becomes a hero in the New World Order. Wild. A whole new energy. Capitalism restored. A happy ending. Or is it?"

And so they found themselves a year and half later, in June 1993, headed toward a different Russia to mount a new production of Brecht's *Threepenny Opera*.

True, Hal's American salesmanship had swayed her, but there was something else as well. A return. Irene had made a trip to the Soviet Union once before, during the Brezhnev years, a cultural trip sponsored by the British Council meant to impress all parties with everybody's mutual goodwill and open-mindedness. They were supposed to meet and exchange ideas with Soviet actors and playwrights who had been handpicked by the party and had no interest whatsoever in the English avant-garde. The Soviets were skeptical, at best, about what they'd heard, and considered most contemporary English theater vulgar and self-indulgent. They were particularly incensed by a discussion of Peter Brook's production of *Marat/Sade*, which they hadn't seen. Never mind. The very idea was counterrevolutionary, they cried.

Despite official Soviet disapproval, Irene had felt welcomed. People had been gracious; they'd shown an interest. Russia, Leningrad in particular, touched Irene more deeply than anything else in her life, though what, exactly, and why, she couldn't say.

It was not politics; that was clear. Like most Western leftists in those days, Irene had felt far and away superior to Communist Party members. Her ideals were loftier and more mutable, based on whim, she'd have to admit now. She had been a firebrand with the Glasgow Repertory, willing to do almost anything in almost any kind of production. The idea was to shock and alarm the middle classes whenever possible—in fact, not to conform to any established mode of thought at all. She bounded naked across the stage in plays that didn't make any sense. She marched in the front line of whichever mass demonstration was on at the moment. Not that she hadn't believed in what she was doing. She believed. Passionately. That's why it surprised her to feel so blunted in middle age. This tour, she supposed, was some last, mad fling before she settled into semi-retirement in Bournemouth.

"All right, love?"

Arthur was at her side.

"Yes, darling," she said. "Remember the Maoist?"

"Pardon?"

"That Chinese opera we did in Liverpool. The director who fancied himself a Maoist. Didn't make any distinction between the peasant's role in the revolution and the artist's. Wanted to send me to work on a farm. You remember."

"Vaguely."

"Well, I'm feeling that way again, Arthur."

"What way is that?"

"Caught in the terrible gulf between art and life."

"Ah, yes," said Arthur, "the terrible gulf."

"Don't tease."

"Sorry, love."

"Never mind," she said. "Just get this blasted train moving again, will you?"

3.

It was past five in the morning when Yuri pressed Irene's shoulder to wake her. She'd been snoring. Startled, she looked him full in the face. She lifted the shade and gazed into her own reflection in the black glass.

"What is it?" she said. "Have we arrived?"

"We walk now," said Yuri.

"But where's the station?" said Irene.

"Far from here. Soon carts will come for baggage."

"But why?" she said. "This is absurd."

Molly was down the corridor, waking the other actors. Arthur stood all buttoned up and ready to go.

"We've broken down," he said. "They're putting us on another train."

Lil, Brian, and the other actors emerged from their compartments with their belongings.

"What about the luggage?" shouted Burt.

"Yuri has assured us it will all be taken care of. *Nyet problema.*" Arthur beamed, full of good nature.

All fatherly radiance drained from him, however, when he stepped back into his compartment and saw Irene squaring her shoulders to face Yuri, who was a good five inches shorter than she.

"I am not leaving this train until we've pulled into a station," she said.

"Irene," said Arthur, "the plumbing's gone."

"What plumbing! The loo's nothing but a hole in the floor!"

"They've got to move the train off the tracks, Irene. We're in danger of causing a wreck. They're going to haul it back to Lithuania or something. We're to get on another train in the next village."

Irene bit her lip. She stood for a moment, then grabbed her handbag from the seat and her jacket from its hook by the door.

"All right, then," she said, glaring down at Yuri.

She marched into the corridor. When she reached the door that would have led to the platform, had there been one, she pushed it open, stepped out, and landed facedown in the mud.

By the time men arrived with torches, she was screaming and hurling fistfuls of earth at the side of the train.

4.

Never in all her life had Irene been so relieved as she was when the military transport lorry stopped, and the young soldiers hopped out and began unloading the bags. This, then, was the hotel: a long, sooty granite building about six stories tall. The sky was clearing. It was late afternoon, and they'd reached Leningrad.

Irene was covered with dried mud. An ornately coifed Russian woman took her out of the queue at the front desk. She plucked Irene's passport from her hand and thrust it toward Yuri. Then she smiled and motioned for Irene to follow her, which Irene did, gladly, up red-carpeted stairs and down brown-carpeted hallways, until the woman opened a door to a room with two beds, a bath, two chairs, a writing table, and crimson plastic hangers on a rod just inside the door. The woman ushered Irene in, put her bags down, and embraced her. Irene hadn't even caught her name. The woman stepped into the bathroom and began filling the tub. When Irene tried to pay her, she shooed her away, as if insulted. She took Irene's hand and led her into the bathroom to show her that the water was getting warm. Then she bowed slightly and disappeared, leaving Irene alone.

This was the Russia Irene remembered and longed for: fierce, gracious, and motherly. Reassured, she took off her clothes and stepped into the warm, rusty water.

5.

Arthur was glad to find Irene asleep when he got to the room some hours later. After registering, he'd stopped for a bite to eat and a drink with Yuri in the grill-bar on the second floor, where they would be taking their meals. They'd talked about football, mostly, which bored Arthur stupid, but he found it useful to keep track of the English teams and their rivals on the Continent because it was a handy topic of conversation, especially with foreigners, and men rarely talked about much else in the beginning. He'd been a dismal failure when he'd played at school, but he knew all the positions and the nomenclature and could summon the necessary enthusiasm. He was, after all, an actor.

Arthur was delighted when Yuri shifted the conversation away from sport and onto the bizarre state of the Russian economy, not that Arthur was any more interested in economics than sport, but it meant the conversation would continue. Two years earlier, a dollar bought about ten rubles, Yuri explained. Today, it bought about a thousand. And prices had risen accordingly. He told Arthur about a baseball team a fellow in Leningrad had started which was already defunct; they hadn't enough money for uniforms.

"Co-ed naked American baseball," cried Arthur, remembering a T-shirt he'd once seen.

Yuri smiled and refilled Arthur's glass.

From football to the economy to baseball, with a nod at politics, which Yuri simply ignored, they landed in the murky territory of philosophical speculation, dead in the middle of the Russian metaphysical quagmire. Though any mention of the invisible usually irked Arthur, he felt he had, at last, arrived. For surely this was, somehow, the real Russia.

He sat watching Irene sleep as he removed his dusty shoes and peeled off his socks.

Yuri was a splendid chap. Irene had something against him though. They'd got off to a bad start. Arthur resolved to plead Yuri's case, for if things didn't improve, Irene could make not just Yuri but everyone else in the company miserable.

"You are married with Irene?" Yuri had asked.

"Oh, no," said Arthur.

"I see," said Yuri.

But he'd got it all wrong. True, they shared a room, they always had whenever they worked together outside London, but they'd never been lovers. Even when one or the other was between marriages or recovering from the sting of a bad love affair, it had never really occurred to either one of them, which, he knew, seemed odd to people, so he didn't try to explain it now. Besides, he could tell Yuri was impressed that Arthur was with such a handsome and difficult woman. He felt it gave him a leg up, somehow, and though Yuri was a hard one to read, Arthur reckoned he was a bit in awe of Irene.

In her mid-fifties, Irene was even more beautiful than she'd been at twenty. Arthur noticed her untroubled face, now, as she slept, her breathing deep and even. Hers was a big, raw beauty. She had masses of unruly reddish-blond hair, now lined with gray and flashes of bright white. Her directness had always caught one off guard. Even today, she strode into rehearsal like a man.

Directors had learned to give her a lot of leeway, for she had a knack, a genius, really, for finding a new way of playing a character. Years ago, she'd phoned him from rehearsal one afternoon.

"I was brilliant, Arthur! When I gave out the herbs, I grabbed each handful from between my legs. It's a mad scene, for God's sake. I've rescued poor old Ophelia from generations of half-wits and waifs. I've found the energy she needs to destroy herself. Otherwise, who knows? She may just as well have stumbled into the river, tripped on a root or something, instead of jumping."

After a good notice in *The Guardian*, she had asked for the same salary as Hamlet. The management refused, so she went back to her dressing room after curtain calls and quietly snipped all of her costumes to ribbons with a pair of pinking shears. Into what was left of a pale blue satin snood, she tucked a note—resigning. She'd felt confident enough then, but when she learned soon thereafter that *Vogue* had called the theater for an interview, she felt invincible.

For all its ups and downs, Irene's career had been far more distinguished than Arthur's. She'd have a fight with an important director, get bad reviews, and then disappear. A season or two later she'd be back in London, doing something brilliant. Her influence, when she had it, was strong enough to net Arthur a small part in a West End production or the occasional film, but mostly he stayed where he was happiest: in regional repertory companies and the Christmas pantomimes.

It was Irene who'd gotten him this job, and he'd come in part because he needed a break and in part because he was curious about this Velvet Revolution. He'd seen them dancing on the Berlin Wall on television, and everyone was talking about a new Russia. Though he'd never been one to fly to the scene of history in the making—that was Irene's department, even when she was there by mistake—it occurred to him that this might be his last chance. He felt about this as he had never felt about anything before, and yet if anyone had asked him, he'd have been hard-pressed to put it into words.

He stood up and finished undressing. It took him a moment to find his pajamas. He brushed his teeth, and before he slipped into his bed (Irene had turned down the covers for him), he kissed her lightly on the side of her head.

6.

Molly punched her pillow and sat up in bed. She couldn't sleep. It was Irene's fault; she'd tricked Molly again. Or it was Molly's own fault for being duped over and over again, which only made her madder.

Here's how it happened. Irene Donovan asked a favor. She'd begin with flattery: "Molly, you're the only woman for the job." Molly would take time to think about it, then usually decline. Irene's standard comeback: "Oh, but Molly! There is no one, *no* one but you!" Sometimes Molly stood firm for days. Then Irene would seduce her; there was no other word for it. Flowers arrived, boxes of chocolate. Molly would succumb to dinners in expensive restaurants and long, intimate talks, for which, as an American in London, she was starved. Apart from her analyst, Irene was the only one in whom Molly confided. Irene's life fascinated Molly, but she couldn't see what Irene gained from their friendship—except, of course, a company manager, an assistant director, or a stage manager for whatever play Irene was in that needed one. In the beginning Molly had been grateful for the work, but now that she was established, she hardly needed it; she turned down work all the time. It was Irene she couldn't refuse, no matter how ill-fated the notion of taking *Hamlet* to Iran, for example, in the years when even the mention of regicide was punishable by death. They both knew, despite the intricate dance toward and away, that Molly would give in.

True, Molly had always wanted to come to Russia. Her freshman year at college she'd fallen in with a group of Trotskyites whom she liked because they tended toward the obscure and could carry a grudge longer than anyone she'd ever met. She loved the stories they told about their hero, his lack of any sense of direction and losing the troops he was trying to lead. His brilliant military and political strategies, which, alas, were not brilliant enough; his affairs with women; his martyrdom in Mexico. To Molly, he was a high romantic figure whom everyone misunderstood, which is how Molly tended to see herself, though she'd never admit it, for she prized above all else her good sense and stability, and the gift she had for managing impossible people.

When Irene happened to mention she was going to Russia with this production of *Threepenny Opera*, Molly held her breath, only for an instant, but long enough so Irene could tell she was interested. Irene had gotten sneakier over the years. She didn't ask right away. In fact, Molly had pretty much forgotten about it three weeks later when she was on her way to Irene's for supper.

It was July and hot, unusually hot for London, and when Irene opened the door to her flat, she was wearing nothing but sandals and an apron, the kind that tied up around the neck.

"You don't mind, do you?" said Irene. "It's just so hot."

"N-no," Molly sputtered. "No, of course not."

Irene took the bottle of wine Molly had brought and went

into the kitchen to open it. All through the salmon salad, the salade Niçoise, the two different fruit sorbets, and the Fortnum and Mason biscuits, Molly's eyes kept alighting on Irene's bare shoulder and sliding down her arm to the breast. Then she'd force herself to look at Irene's face, less often and more slowly toward the end of the second bottle of wine. Everything about Irene's body was strong, vivid, not the least bit self-conscious. Molly kept her black T-shirt and jeans on. Even her shoes and socks.

"So. How about it?" said Irene, leaning forward, her chin cupped in her hand.

Molly's eyes widened. "How about what?"

"We need a company manager for the tour next year. Prague, Warsaw, Leningrad. Twelve weeks. We'd be back early in August."

"Oh, no," said Molly, "not with Hal behind it."

"What's the matter with Hal?"

"You know damn well. He's the kiss of death."

"But he's brilliant; you've seen his work."

"The man's impossible."

"He is a bit, isn't he?"

"A *bit*?"

"But the work, Molly. The work is splendid."

"Uneven. He's done some appalling things. Too much depends on his boyfriend at the time. *And* he's a liar."

A faraway light came into Irene's eyes, a challenge, really, that said she was determined to sail no matter who was at the helm or how dangerous the waters. It was a look both mystical and belligerent and, once again, it dared Molly to come along. And, once again (they both knew), Molly would follow, though she'd pretend to hold out for another couple of days.

Molly punched the pillow again, hissing, "Damn. Damn.

Damn."

A sharp knock came at the door. Molly stopped, her fists in midair. She held her breath. It was another door, not hers. It had to be. But it wasn't. She heard it again; the knock was softer this time. One of the actors, she thought. She leaped up, threw on her robe, and opened the door.

It was Yuri. His face was all screwed up in an expression that made her want to laugh.

"What's the matter?" they both whispered at once.

"The noise. The cries. I thought you were in danger," he said.

"I couldn't sleep," said Molly. "You know how it is."

Yuri cocked his head and pulled a bottle of Georgian wine from behind his back. "Perhaps this could help." He moved forward with a little half smile. Molly wanted to punch his face.

Instead, she said, "Good night," and closed the door.

7.

By the time Molly walked into the grill-bar the next morning, the actors were already seated, waiting for breakfast. Molly was so tired, she had to focus a minute to recognize Susan, who wore a light-blue silk blouse, a salmon-colored scarf, and layers of complicated makeup. They'd been traveling together six weeks, and Susan had not yet exhausted her wardrobe (her war chest, Burt called it). She was a pretty young woman, tall, thin, blond, from the Midwest, and there was something aggressive, almost hostile, about the way she dressed and made herself up. Or so it seemed to Molly, who wore one of two pairs of jeans she'd brought and a clean T-shirt under a loose-fitting cotton shirt. She was always dressed for work, which usually included mucking around backstage, especially on this tour. Molly had been hired as stage (and company) manager by Hal, the producer, whose loyal assistant, apologist, and onetime boyfriend was supposed to direct, but he'd been hospitalized in London the day before they left with an emergency appendectomy, so it fell to Molly to direct the play as well. She'd done it all before, but never all at once.

"Morning," said Arthur.

"Isn't it good to be off that train?" said Irene. "You look as if you hadn't slept a wink."

"I didn't," said Molly. "Or at least not much."

"Poor love," said Irene. "Let's get you some coffee."

"Guilty conscience?" said Burt.

"Haven't had time to do anything my conscience would object to," said Molly, as she sat in the last empty chair at the table.

She liked Burt; they all did. He claimed he'd become an actor by mistake. There were never enough men trying out for college productions, so his girlfriends (actresses, invariably) dragged him along to auditions, and he usually got a part, so that in his senior year at the University of Colorado, when he had to choose between an interview with an engineering firm and an audition for *Curse of the Starving Class*, he chose the latter, and he'd been doing it ever since: crisscrossing the States in regional productions, doing commercials and voice-overs when he could get them, until he'd come to London on vacation a year ago, auditioned for Mack the Knife, and got the part.

Molly was afraid Yuri would mention something about the noise coming from her room the night before, but all he said was "Good morning."

She nodded, and smiled rather more genuinely than she intended, out of relief.

"Isn't anyone going to ask how *I* slept?" said Susan.

"Of course, my darling," cooed Irene. "How did you sleep?"

"Fine" was all Susan said and went back to buttering a thin slice of black bread.

Brian and Lil rolled their eyes at each other. They made Molly think of Jack Sprat and his wife. Brian was long and lanky, about as laid-back as anyone could be. Lil was pretty and plump and prone to depression, and whatever conflict there'd been between them in Warsaw, Molly noticed, seemed to be over.

"Well, I certainly feel better," said Irene. "And I must apologize for my behavior last night. I was overwrought. A nice bath and a good night's sleep—that's what was wanted. By the way, Yuri, the hotel staff seems to have disappeared. I couldn't find anyone to fetch me clean towels this morning."

"Holiday?" said Yuri.

"Don't *you* go off on holiday," said Arthur.

"No," said Yuri. "You have my divided loyalty. Be assured. I am no turnface."

Coat, thought Molly, turn*coat*, but she thought better of correcting him. Everyone was in a good mood, and with luck it would carry them through what might be a tough spot: this morning's rehearsal, their first with the Russian cast members.

"Did you get the actors and musicians we need?" asked Molly.

"Sure, yes, of course," said Yuri. "The actors will be at rehearsal hall sharply at nine thirty. The musicians you will meet tomorrow. They know their parts perfectly. You have only to direct them."

Breakfast came. Eggs cooked in metal dishes with tomato. Kasha. A small potato-and-fish salad. Black and white bread with butter and delicious jam. Fruit juice called *sok*. The moment a cup was empty, a waitress was there with fresh coffee or tea. Another large, blond lady presided over the staff, barking orders, turning to smile at the actors once in a while, smoothing the front of her skirt, as if she were about to bow slightly. As they were leaving, she asked Yuri in Russian if everything had been all right. She had Yuri tell the actors to let her know if they needed anything, anything at all, for it was an honor, she said, to serve such distinguished artists of the theater.

8.

The idea was to engage local actors in each city they visited. Then they'd gather simple props with the help of people from the community. In this way, it was a collaborative effort.

Yuri had secured an auditorium with a stage in a vast, plum-colored building, a palace one of the tzars built for his brother or a mistress. Under the Communists, it had housed an institute whose purpose no one really knew. Now it was one of Leningrad's many new cultural centers, the site of foreign conferences on parapsychology or marketing, more often than not launching some hopeful and ill-fated joint venture.

The seven men Yuri had gathered milled around onstage, talking among themselves in Russian. One held his cap in his hand. Another stood, staring at his own boots. A man with one arm looked up at the carved figures of men and women turning to gaze out of the stone columns. A blond man with one blind eye joked with the man standing to his left. And a tall, lean, handsome man with black hair and a long scar on his cheek was already flirting with Susan, who was, of course, flirting back.

He hasn't a chance, thought Irene, watching them. Not in the long run, he hasn't. Not with Susan. Irene reckoned he was after American citizenship, a fast-food franchise in Los Angeles, perhaps, which meant marriage, and Susan was not—at least from what Irene could see—the marrying sort. She loved the chase and the thrill of conquest too much to settle into domestic bliss. And she was not, certainly not, the sort who fell in love with misery for its own sake; she was too self-absorbed and flighty. No, if Susan married at all, Irene reckoned, it would be late in life, once she'd exhausted every other possibility and succumbed, finally, to complete despair.

Molly was astonished by how much these guys looked like actual thieves and beggars. Not so the three women Yuri had found. They were young, slender, and carefully made-up. One was dressed in a kind of suit for the office; the other two looked as if they were on their way to the disco.

"All right," said Molly. "Good morning. Thank you for coming. My name is Molly Soule; I'm directing you in this play. You've all had a chance to read the script. Yes? … Good. So you have a sense of what it's about. Can everyone understand me? Yes? Good. Speak up if you can't. Don't be afraid to ask questions. Yuri can always act as interpreter.

"Now. I'd like to begin with an exercise in mime—no words— to warm up. We'll start with act one, scene two: the wedding of Mack the Knife and Polly Peachum. I'll call out the moves, and you walk through them, using whatever gestures seem to make sense to you. Big gestures. Really exaggerate. Have fun with it. This is satire. Burlesque. Not *Boris Godunov*."

Silence. They all looked terrified, except for the tall dark man with the scar across his cheek. He laughed.

"I want you to look for these characters in your body," Molly continued. "How do they move? Where do they feel their tension? Now. The tall gentleman."

"I am Sasha," he said.

"Good. Sasha. I'd like you to play Matthew today. And I'd

like you, sir," she said, pointing, "yes, the gentleman with the cap. What is your name, please?"

"I am Ivan Alexeievitch."

"Ivan, would you play Filch this morning? The rest of you simply respond when I say 'Gang.' Okay? The other women aren't in this scene, so could you come out front, please? Thank you. *Spaseeba.*"

Sasha, as Matthew, crouched and spun around, pointing his finger like a revolver, as if he'd done it every day of his life. Burt, as Macheath, and Susan, as Polly, entered and looked around. Sasha stopped and put a hand to his ear to indicate the arrival of the wagon outside.

"Gang!" shouted Molly, and in came the thugs bearing gifts: an invisible harpsichord, carpets, silver candelabra, a Renaissance sofa. Susan mimed crying because the goods were stolen. Burt silently scolded the men for not stealing better stuff. And the men defended themselves by pleading with open arms and urgent faces.

Then they all took their seats at the invisible table and began eating in a manner so wild and uproarious that everybody burst out laughing.

"Great!" said Molly. "That brings us up to 'Pirate Jenny'; we'll skip the songs for today. Now. Whoever eventually plays Walter announces Tiger Brown, Sheriff of London. Gang creeps away. Enter Brian, as Brown. Greet Macheath. That's right; you're old friends. Okay, good. That brings us to 'Song of the Heavy Cannon.' Exit Brown and Macheath. Matthew and … you," she said, pointing to the one-armed man, "would you mind playing Walter for a minute? Thank you. Confer with Polly. Good. Yes. Now, Gang assembles behind a hanging carpet. Just move to the back for now. That's it. Then Gang, you'll sing 'Wedding

Song for Poorer People.'

"Now Macheath tears down the carpet. Exit Gang. No. Let's try splitting you in two groups; half exit stage left, the other half stage right. Yes. I like that better. Which leaves Macheath and Polly to sing their duet at the end of the scene. Wonderful. Thanks very much. Now let's take it from the beginning again."

Watching Molly work with the men, Irene was astonished by how natural they seemed. Born actors, she supposed. Or actual thieves.

9.

They broke for lunch at one. Back at the hotel, the grill-bar staff had prepared a small feast, beautifully set out for them with vases of peonies. The tables were pushed together to accommodate the whole group. They'd even turned off the television. The Russians toasted the American and English actors, the Americans toasted the Russians, Arthur toasted Yuri and then Irene, Irene toasted Molly, and, as they were finishing dessert, everyone stood to toast the grill-bar staff, who, in their turn, applauded the actors.

They had the afternoon free. The women excused themselves to sleep off the toasts. The Russian actors disappeared. Irene announced she was going for a walk. Molly felt slighted that she wasn't asked to come along. After a few cups of strong coffee, Yuri took the men to see the Hermitage.

They reeled through rooms of silver and ball gowns and coaches and Fabergé eggs. Yuri did his best to give them the official information, since they'd decided not to hire a guide. The men did their best to act interested, but they were half drunk and giddy and made jokes about Catherine the Great's sexual appetite, rumors that Yuri did nothing to dispel, though Arthur wondered if Yuri didn't take offense, somehow.

Then they stepped into a large gallery with nothing but military portraits.

"Well, here they are," said Arthur.

Yuri went around, telling stories about some of the generals and their wars, and was about to lead them into the next room, when Burt launched into song: "*What soldiers live on …*" Arthur and the others joined in:

> "*Is heavy cannon*
> *From the Cape to Cutch Behar.*
> *If it should rain one night*
> *And they should chance to sight*
> *Pallid or swarthy faces*
> *Of uncongenial races*
> *They'll maybe chop them up to make some beefsteak tartare.*"

Burt continued solo:

> "*John's gone west and James is dead*
> *And George is missing and barmy.*
> *Blood, however, is still blood red:*
> *They're recruiting again for the army.*"

Then all of them, together, much louder:

> "*What soldiers live on*
> *Is heavy cannon*
> *From the Cape to Cutch Behar.*
> *If it should rain one night*
> *And they should chance to sight—*"

But before they could actually name what they should chance to sight, they were surrounded by stout women in dusty black dresses—museum guards—one at the right and left elbow of each man. As they were frog-marched through one gallery after another, Arthur stopped laughing and said, "All right, then, we'll leave. You needn't—"

Yuri hissed at the guards, then shouted at them. About what, Arthur could only guess. Burt and the others walked along briskly, trying to keep up with their escorts, who, Arthur noticed, marched with an agility one rarely finds in the aged. Outside, they were handed over to the police. The men wisely left all further negotiations to Yuri, who, after showing the officer various forms of identification, put his hand behind his back and brushed his fingers over his thumb.

"Money!" cried Arthur. "A bribe! Is that all? Why didn't you say so, constable?" He pulled a hundred-ruble note from his wallet.

Yuri's hand closed and wagged back and forth.

"He wants hard currency," said Brian, pulling a ten-dollar bill from his wallet. Sure enough, Yuri grabbed it and brought his hand around, not once but twice more (there were three policemen), so that in the end he'd collected ten dollars from each of the actors.

Arthur wondered how Yuri could tell the difference between rubles and dollars with his back turned.

Walking into the sunlight to hail a cab, Arthur noticed a collared bear stepping from one foot to the other when prodded by a man who held his rope. The bear looked hot and weary, with his muzzle turned skyward. White foam gathered at the edges of his mouth. The man shouted at passersby to look at this amazing dancing bear. He kept pushing a short stick into the bear's ribs. Back and forth, the bear swayed.

At the end of another rope held by the same man, a monkey sat on a railing and nibbled a nut. Just then, it cocked its head and stared at Arthur.

10.

Even before Irene heard the woman cry out, she knew she was American, or at least not Russian. Something about the gesture. She stood with her arms outstretched, a bridal bouquet in one hand, her veil tossed back over her head. A bridesmaid (Irene supposed) stood at her side. The bride smiled as if to show off her straight, white teeth (American, she had to be) and waited for the photographer to take the picture.

The first odd thing Irene noticed was that the bride was being photographed not in front of a national monument, which Irene understood to be the custom in Russia, but out here in the middle of a park, in front of a pond. The second thing that struck her as odd was that the bride stood with a bridesmaid and not the groom. In fact, the groom, his men friends, and a few young boys were at that moment, the moment the photographer must have opened the shutter, running away from the bride and toward the pond, where two men were hauling a large body onto the grass.

The only other sound was an aria Irene didn't recognize coming from a radio on a nearby blanket, and then the plaintive cry of the American bride: "Misha? Where are you? Misha, the photographer's waiting. MisSHaaaA!"

11.

Some days later, when Molly came around the corner to the canal side of the palace, she found the Russian actors unloading a truck.

"Wonderful!" she cried. "Where did you find all the furniture?"

"Most is borrowed," said Yuri, grabbing the end of a Renaissance couch, "donated by lovers of the theater."

"Make sure to give me a list of their names," she said, "so I can put aside complimentary tickets. A harpsichord! My God! I can't believe this."

Molly grabbed the sagging middle of a rolled-up Persian carpet carried by Ivan and the one-armed actor. Once inside the building, she began making a list of props she needed, checking it against the list of things she'd brought.

"Hey Yuri," she called. "Any chance of locating a stage revolver? You know, a gun, something like a pistol. Plastic would do. It doesn't get fired."

Yuri put down the chest of silver he was carrying and addressed the actors in Russian. They laughed and each in his turn pulled from inside his jacket a gun and raised it into the air, as if about to fire. Lil fairly leaped into Brian's arms. Like an American Western, thought Irene.

"Christ!" shouted Molly. "Put those away. What the hell are you carrying guns for?"

"The critics, I should think," said Arthur.

"I want a stage gun. Fake. Harmless. Get it?"

A fat bald man Molly had never seen before stepped out of the shadows. He emptied his own pistol of bullets and tossed it to Molly, who caught it in one hand.

"It's empty," he said. "It will hurt no one. Use it. Please. Be my guest."

"No," said Molly. She tossed it back to him. "We'll improvise. We'll use a stick of wood if we have to. There'll be no guns in this theater. Yuri, make that clear to everybody."

The strange man turned and spoke to the men in Russian. Some put their hands up, while others frisked them, only to reveal smaller guns and bullets strapped to their calves. Yuri went around collecting the weapons in a cardboard box.

"From now on," said Molly, "if I catch anyone with any kind of weapon, I'm calling the police."

The men chuckled, translating what Molly had said among themselves. Ivan cringed in mock fear. Sasha simply put his hands on his hips and roared with laughter.

The bald stranger yelled at them, and they fell silent.

"Who the hell *are* you?" said Molly.

"Forgive me. I did not introduce myself. My name is Mikhail Sergeyevich. You will have no more troubles with these fellows. I assure you. Please continue with your work."

"I'm Molly Soule, the director. I'd invite you to stay, but putting a production like this together is really quite private."

"Like a love affair," he said, smacking his lips.

"Perhaps," said Molly.

They shook hands, then he bowed and left.

"All right," she said. "Let's take it from the opening of act one, scene two. The wedding. Songs and all. Places everybody."

Sasha leaped onto the stage, carrying a lantern and pointing his index finger like a gun: "Hi! Hands up, if anyone's there!"

Burt, as Macheath, entered and came to the front of the stage: "Well? Is anyone here?"

Sasha: "Not a soul. We can have our marriage here safe enough."

Susan entered as Polly, Mack's bride-to-be: "But this is a stable!"

By midnight, they'd only gotten through the second scene of act two.

"All right," said Molly. "Let's stop here. You've been terrific. I mean it. Thank you. Let's get some sleep and meet back here at nine tomorrow for the last four scenes. Then we'll take the rest of the day off. Anything anyone needs to say before we break? Any questions?"

"Yes," said Sasha. "Why is it the Russians have such small parts in the play? What kind of collaboration is this? Where all the starring roles goes to Westerners, and Russians play *hooliganski?*"

"And besides this, the play makes no sense," said the blond man with one blind eye. "It's all contradictions."

"And why must we Russian women play prostitutes? It's an insult," said a short, redheaded actress.

"Wait a minute, wait a minute," said Molly. "One at a time. Look. If there were time for you to learn the bigger parts, I'd have loved to cast you in them, especially now that I've seen your work. But we have hardly any rehearsal time as it is. So it's a practical concern, really. I don't mean any offense by it. As for the relative virtue of the characters, look at Macheath, our hero. He's a murderer, a thief, a philanderer."

"What, please, means 'phi-land—'?" asked the Russian with one arm.

"A womanizer. He cheats on his new wife."

"Not such a good woman," said the redheaded actress.

"That's just the point. The characters are full of contradictions. We all are. Brecht's aim was to get us to see ourselves critically. He exposed corruption for what it is: something we all live out to varying degrees in the course of our lives."

"If Macheath is the hero and a lover, should he not be played by a strong, handsome man such as myself?" said Sasha.

"But that's just it," said Molly. "Macheath is meant to be a businessman, a petit bourgeois, not a romantic hero. When people come to the theater and see heroes and villains in the old style, they know just what to expect, so they sit back and fall asleep. Brecht wants to wake us up. Somewhere he says that in early English drawings, Macheath had 'a head like a radish.' "

"Thanks a lot," said Burt.

"Seriously. Brecht challenges our expectations; he turns the world upside down. We're surprised. We're uncomfortable. We laugh ourselves awake."

"But he offers no solutions," said Ivan.

"Exactly," said Molly. "That's why we brought the play back into this new context of post-Communist Russia. To see what it would reflect. Isn't it enough to be caught off guard, to be outraged, and then to recognize ourselves? Not for any moral rehabilitation but to admit, once again, that we're human. Then? Who knows what we do with it, what happens when we leave the theater and go back to our lives. That's the mystery."

12.

But she knew nothing about it, really, Molly thought later, trying to sleep. Not outside Sheridan, Shaw, Chekhov. Not outside political theory or what she'd observed. Romance, lovers, the life to which one returned when one walked out the stage door. For that's what was meant by one's life, and Molly knew nothing about it. The theater was her life: single-minded devotion to work. Discipline. Uncluttered by personal concerns. People urged her to date. People said she ought to get a cat. It infuriated her: the presumption that work, friends, a private life of the mind weren't enough. They were. They had to be.

"Are you quite sure?" her analyst had said some months earlier in London.

"What makes you think I'm not?" said Molly.

"What brought you to analysis three years ago?"

"Nightmares. Insomnia. Anxiety."

"Yes. Your fears were bigger than you were. You've conquered most of them, haven't you? And it's true, you love your work, but you've also said you're lonely in a way others can't seem to touch. As skeptical as you are about people in love, I still wonder if you don't envy them just a little."

Molly started to say something, then stopped.

After a moment, she said, "I hate how they go on and on about it; that's all. I get to feeling incapable, somehow, as if it weren't my choice, as if I'd failed."

"Or done something wrong?"

"Maybe," said Molly.

But it wasn't that; it was more a failure of the imagination. She could imagine the placement of props and actors on a stage easily enough, even imagine the psychological impact. And she advised the actors in their personal lives based on some sort of sympathetic imagination, she supposed. But she could not imagine for herself a courtship, the wooing or being wooed.

"Have you never had sexual fantasies?" asked her analyst.

"Not as such," said Molly.

"What do you mean?" said the analyst.

"I don't know. Sometimes when I'm very tired, I imagine walking out the stage door. I just keep walking through the city, past the suburbs. Soon I'm in a meadow, and then a desert, no houses or fences anywhere. I keep walking toward a mountain

on the horizon in the far-off distance. I walk until I'm so tired
I lie down right where I am, resigned to my fate, and wait for
the buzzards. Then I see my bones, years later, blazed bright
white by the sun."

"I see," said the analyst.

Molly searched her mind for something better; she felt inad-
equate. She wanted to say she could imagine being cared for
if she had the flu or something. She thought of conversations
with Irene. She tried to imagine touching her, but she could
not reach certain moments, could not picture, for instance, a
first kiss, and she was suddenly ashamed.

It was that one had to give up everything. It was an annihi-
lation! She wanted to say. But the analytic hour was over.

At thirty-nine, she was still a virgin.

When she did sleep that night, she dreamed she was on
the Metro, and a drunk Russian man in dirty old clothes was
eating a cucumber, swaying back and forth, mumbling, until
the chicken he had tucked under one arm slipped to the floor,
and he started cursing and kicking the chicken, stomping on
it with demonic energy. When the doors opened, she saw the
procession she'd seen from the broken-down train. They were
dressed in silks and veils and embroidered coats. She heard the
bells sewn into their clothes and their singing and murmuring.

In the dream, she followed them at a distance at first and
then fell in with them, joined them, heard her own voice sing
something low in her throat. Up the stairs they went, out of
the Metro station, through the streets of Leningrad, until they
reached the seashore, and there before them was a canopy of
white silk on four posts set in a square. Two figures stood under
it, bride and bridegroom, their backs to the procession. For a
moment all was silent, until the sound of glass breaking, muffled

under a cloth, under first the bride's foot and then the groom's.

13.

"You're English," said the woman standing next to her.

"Yes, I am," said Irene. "Is it that obvious?" She turned to the pale woman looking up at her. Mid-thirties, she guessed.

"It's the shoes. I almost bought the same pair at Harrods when I was home at Christmastime."

The woman wore a simple dark dress, sleeveless. She had slender arms. Her blond hair was tucked into what looked to be a Liberty's silk square, deep blue with lavender paisley. She had a beautiful complexion and pale blue eyes, terribly alert.

"I take it you're not here on holiday," said Irene.

"No," said the woman. "I'm researching a book."

"What about?"

"Organized crime."

"Sounds dangerous," said Irene.

"Everything is dangerous in this country," the woman said. "My name is Amanda Peters."

"Irene Donovan," she said, extending her hand. "I'm an actress. We're here doing *Threepenny Opera*."

They stood in front of a woman selling cherries in a covered market. Amanda offered a cherry to Irene to sample and ate one herself. They nodded to each other, and Amanda went ahead and filled a small paper sack with them.

As they walked along together past stalls of fish and fruit, Irene described some of their difficulties on this tour.

"And to make matters worse, some poor, lovesick girl wanted to join us in Warsaw. Then our train broke down somewhere between Vilnius and Leningrad, so we had to walk to the nearest village and rode in on military lorries. Just the other day, we learned that all the local actors carry guns."

"Welcome to the new Russia," said Amanda.

"I'm beginning to think I liked the old Russia better," said Irene.

"When were you here last?"

"Twenty years ago."

"The Brezhnev years," said Amanda. "In some ways preferable to the present day. Not in most ways. I came here first as a student of Russian literature some years ago and again later as a consultant for joint business ventures. Things have changed so fast. I used to think I knew Russia. Now I'm not so sure. Six weeks ago, I was standing outside a hotel, telling a joke to some Russian friends. All of a sudden, I had two policemen escorting me to their car. They threw me in the backseat and drove off. I was under arrest, they explained, not because they thought I was a prostitute, which they did, but because I hadn't paid them off yet. The whole incident was actually a compliment to my proficiency in Russian. In telling the joke, I'd used a vulgar expression not found in the phrase books. And because a Russian woman talking to men in front of a hotel signals prostitution, and because they didn't recognize me as having paid my bribe, I was under arrest. In the old days you only had to bribe one bloke, a party official usually. Now you have to bribe everyone along the way, sort of like value-added tax. When I showed the police my press card, they took me back to the hotel straightaway and let me out without another word."

"Incredible," said Irene.

"It's known as the criminalization of Russian society."

"Is that what I feel sometimes in the streets?"

"The way people turn round to see who's following?" said

Amanda.

"Yes," said Irene. "I don't remember feeling it twenty years ago. I mean, I knew I was being watched, but I felt oddly protected by it. At least as a foreigner."

"Oh, people were afraid then, too, and even if you weren't quite sure who the enemy was, you usually knew who your friends were. No one knows who to trust anymore. No one's sure who's running the country, who's running the KGB or what it does, or who, in fact, controls the nuclear arsenal."

"And yet," said Irene, "with all that, I feel as if I were falling in love with old women's faces in the Metro, with lilacs, brass bands, the air itself. It's really quite mad."

"I know what you mean," said Amanda. "This is, after all, still Russia. I was enthralled the moment I set foot in Leningrad. Once it has touched you, the soul of this land, I mean really touched you, you're never the same. The next thing you know, you've taken a Russian lover. Not a good idea, really."

"You speak from experience."

"Let's just say … Yes. I'm in a bit of a mess at the moment. May have got myself in too deep this time. You see, I'd planned to interview this fellow, a rather important figure in the Mafia, for the book, and even before I knew it was happening, we were lovers. He doesn't suspect I'm anything but an Englishwoman helping businesses to get established here. He thinks the book is about joint ventures. And because we're … intimate, he tells me a good deal more about how the underworld works than he might ordinarily … by way of explaining how business is conducted here, of course, and to show off for me a bit. I'm taking you into my confidence over this. Do you mind?"

"No," said Irene. "Not at all."

"So I can trust you?"

"Completely," said Irene.

"We're discreet for a number of reasons, not the least of which is that I'm married. Quite happily, I might add. It's nothing to do with this, although I'm not sure what this is really."

"Funny," said Irene. "I don't know what makes me think of this, but when I was here before, I met an actress. She approached me after a panel, said she was interested in talking further. She took me outside, across the street, away from any microphones, and we sat in a little park. Pathetic, really, a few scraggly trees, nothing more than a vacant lot. There was a thicket of older trees we walked toward. It was dark inside the thicket. Druidic, somehow. We talked a bit about the theater, clothes, film, marriage, food. She asked if we might meet again and made me promise to tell no one. She wanted me to carry some letters and post them once I got back to England. If, by chance, a customs officer found them, I was to claim I knew nothing about them or how they got into my luggage. The next afternoon, I complained of menstrual cramps to get out of some excursion or other, and when everyone had gone, I took an indirect route back to the park in case I was being followed. I sat on the bench and waited. After a while, I got up and walked to the thicket of old trees and stood looking out into the open space. Then I went to the edge of the pavement and looked up and down the street. I began to worry I'd got the wrong time. Or she'd been seen with me and arrested. Or this was a trap, and I was in danger. I waited for an hour and a quarter and then went back to the hotel.

"A week or so later, we were standing by the bus that was taking us to the airport, and I saw the woman across the road, watching. When I made a move toward her, she raised her hand, turned, and walked away. I've often wondered what happened.

It's strange, but I half expect to run into her somewhere in Leningrad."

Amanda took Irene's arm as they walked. Near the Metro station, Amanda nodded toward a group of young men leaning against a long black car with tinted windows.

"They're the real up-and-comers," she said, "the ones you want to watch. Being groomed by the old gangsters. They're the future of Russia, if we're not careful."

They looked to Irene like younger versions of the actors Yuri had hired, and she was about to say as much, when she noticed an older fat man climb out of the back of the limo.

"Why, that's Mikhail Sergeyevich," she said.

"You know him?" said Amanda.

"He's come round the theater. At first I thought he was the acting coach for the Russians."

Amanda nudged Irene into a doorway, hidden from view. "He shouldn't see us together," she said. "He's the one I was telling you about."

"Your lover?"

"Yes. I wonder why he's so interested in your theater company?"

"Oh, he's more than interested," said Irene. "Turns out he's the one who arranged the tour, issued the invitation. He's the head of the Janus Society of International Friendship and Understanding Through the Dramatic Arts. He's supplied us with Yuri and the actors and musicians."

"Go back to your hotel. Do you know the way? I'll ring you later. Not a word to anyone, right?"

"Right," said Irene.

14.

Since he was not interested in meeting the same guards who'd tossed him out of the Hermitage on his last afternoon off, Arthur decided to visit the Russian Museum. Alone, this time.

He strolled through room after room of landscapes: rolling hills, fields of wheat. Handsome peasants in their loose blouses, the women in their colorful head scarves. Expanses of snow and winter skies of an unsettling green. Sleighs full of noblemen in fur hats. It was the light, he supposed, that made these paintings unlike the ones he'd seen in the Louvre or the National Gallery. And there was a foreboding in even the most lighthearted scenes. Something in the eyes of the people.

When Yuri told stories about his childhood (he and his parents hunted autumn mushrooms in forests outside Moscow), they seemed to touch history in a way Arthur couldn't quite imagine for himself. Though the harshness of postwar Britain was part of his own boyhood, he never really thought about his life in relation to history. Not ambitious enough, he reckoned. That was Irene's domain: the big picture. History or anything even a few steps removed from what presently occupied his mind seemed impossibly remote to him. And yet to hear Yuri tell it, everything in one's life was a response to some shift in history. One could almost hear the creak of a hinge as one event opened upon another.

Was this, then, one of those moments? The sense that anything could now happen in Russia, the feeling of change, excitement, menace; the very air in Leningrad this summer had fired Arthur's imagination. Or was it Yuri? The time they spent together, his stories, his—but what was it about him? And what was this feeling?

Now he stood before a painting of tables laden with bowls of fruit and vases of flowers. His eyes followed a line of light as it ran around the rim of a samovar, stopped sharp in a glint, and shone there; the same light changed shape and color as it hit an apple broadside and curled in various plump hues around each single grape in a bunch.

He turned. He walked away and stopped off to the side of a large picture of a woman who was so thin she seemed to float above the chair she sat on. "Anna Akhmatova, a famous poet," the guide told a group next to him. Following the group at some distance, Arthur found himself before a huge portrait of a man in a top hat and tailcoat, another man with a bow and arrow at his side. "Meyerhold the theater director," he heard the guide say. Then there was a picture of a man with his old nurse in the background. "Diaghilev." Oh yes, Arthur remembered, the Ballets Russes. And here was a portrait of a large man leaning back, taking tea on a couch. "Shaliapin," said the guide, "a great actor."

Surely there were portraits of Olivier, Richardson, and Gielgud somewhere—in the National Portrait Gallery, he supposed—but he didn't remember having ever seen them. And had anyone bothered to paint portraits of Derek or Alec … or Irene, for that matter?

Arthur let the group move on and sat down. The only other person in the room was a young soldier, medium height and build, strong, lean, fit from military service, Arthur imagined. The soldier stood in front of a portrait of what looked to be a mid-nineteenth-century lady. Nothing about the picture struck Arthur as remarkable. It was the soldier Arthur noticed, the way he stood there, not moving, not even seeming to breathe, just looking and looking into the young lady's face. She was blond and wore a light green hat with a pale yellow ribbon. She looked directly out of the picture. Neither mocking nor provoking. A plain, clear expression. Pleasure, perhaps. Simply that. Curiosity about the world, yes, Arthur could see that in her face, but mostly it was a confidence he suddenly remembered feeling himself when he was nineteen or twenty, a sense that he was approaching his full range, meeting his future with squared shoulders and the best of intentions. The world was going to be marvelous. One was sure of it. London was going to be marvelous. The theater, marriage, friendships were all going to be more marvelous than any of their elders could imagine, for they had grown cautious and jaded, warning one against this or that, holding one back because of their own disappointments. For life made cowards of the old, it was true. But at twenty, at twenty-five, even …

Arthur straightened his spine and noticed that his feet still ached. The young soldier had fallen in love with the lady, or with the painting, it seemed, for he kept on looking at it and didn't move, because it could make him feel this way, make him see in an instant what he'd gone his whole life without noticing until now: this powerful gaze meeting his own from beneath a green hat with a yellow ribbon. A woman long dead. They do die, you know, Arthur wanted to tell him. People disappoint. One falls out of love. But why should he want to interrupt this young soldier's dream, just when he stood, as he now seemed to, on the threshold of some new insight about love, or art, or women?

Let him be, he thought.

Arthur stood and turned to go—it was late, there was rehearsal that evening—and felt a great sorrow in his bones.

15.

"They're charming when they want to be," said Irene. "Romantic, I suppose. But not really sexual, these Russian men, are they?"
She was packing things she'd need for rehearsal.
"I'm not sure I see what you mean," said Arthur.
He was brushing his teeth.
"Take this Yuri, for example. He goes round chatting up each dolly bird he sees, yet it's all rather pro forma, as if he's just doing what's expected of him. Part of his job."
Irene noticed Arthur had cast his glance downward and drawn his lips together (there was toothpaste in his mustache) as if he were about to take issue with what she'd just said. She stopped for a moment to consider Arthur in the mirror and the pitch of his shoulders. She continued, more cautiously now, for she'd hurt him somehow.
"I don't know," she said. "It's just he's hard to read, that's all. I don't trust him. Can't put my finger on it."

16.

"No, no, no," said Molly. "Go back to 'Polly/Lucy loves Mack.' That's where you're going wrong. Do it again, *very* slowly."
Susan and Lil rehearsed their "Jealousy Duet," a fast song they'd had trouble with since the beginning. Burt and Brian sat over a game of chess. Molly had sent the Russian actors and musicians off on a break. Irene yawned. She fingered a loose button on her blouse, then put her elbow on the arm of the chair and rested her chin on her palm. She stared off into the shadowy wings, where she could just barely make out Arthur and another figure (Yuri, she supposed) seated on two chairs

in the dusty gray evening light coming from a window high up
in a wall farther backstage.

"No!" Molly shouted. "Each note has to be distinct, or the
interruptions sound like mush. Try it again. Slow it down even
more."

Irene looked back into the dark wing. Something in the position of Arthur's body made her keep looking. He was slouching
farther and farther back, his legs open.

> SUSAN: *"Who, if either hand were free?"*
> LIL: *"Who, if either hand were free?"*
> SUSAN: *"Would not try that hand on me?"*
> LIL: *"Would not try that hand on me?"*
> SUSAN: *"Ha ha ha ha ha! But for you, Who'd dip his spoon in
> such a stew?"*

Damn, thought Irene, this is going to take all night. When she
turned her attention back to Arthur, his face was gone, obscured
by Yuri's head and shoulders, as if he were telling him something
urgent. But Arthur's hands were on Yuri's back. A kiss. A long
kiss. She looked away to see if anyone else had seen.

Molly had. A moment earlier, she'd followed Irene's glance
and seen Yuri leaning over to kiss, for what else could it have
been? And who else but Arthur? And then, as if the electrical
charge between the two lovers arced over the intervening space,
it shot up Molly's spine, as Lil and Susan sang together, slowly:
"A man will not dissever
A bond that lasts forever
To please some filthy creature!
Ludicrous!!"
That she should see this as a betrayal shocked Molly. Yuri's

flirtations had irritated her. And yet she'd been flattered some-how, happy for the attention; the very thought now made her ashamed.

"Good," said Molly. "Much better. Macheath!" she shouted. "Burt! Let's go on from here."

Burt strode over and resumed his place at the side of Susan and Lil. Irene stood up, ready for her entrance. Brian came and stood beside Irene.

Arthur stepped out of the shadow from behind the scrim, smoothing his mustache, and it struck Molly that the kiss she'd just witnessed held, likely would always hold, more force and veracity than any kiss placed on her own lips.

17.

Irene put cold cream on her face. Arthur read a six-week-old copy of *Variety*. They were getting ready for bed.

"You haven't heard a word I've said."

"I have," said Arthur. "You've seen a horse."

"A corpse, Arthur, not a horse—a *corpse*."

"Another one?"

"That's what I've been trying to tell you, yes. And I've seen him twice."

"It's not a third corpse, then. You're sure."

"Quite certain. The first time, I told you, there were people around. Men hauled him out of a pond. But this second one was lying on the grass in another park."

"Drunk, I should think."

"No," said Irene. "He was dead, all right. I poked him with my umbrella. Then I saw him again today on my walk, and he'd moved; someone had moved him."

Arthur came over and put his hands on Irene's shoulders.

"You've been under a strain," he said.

"Don't patronize me, Arthur. I know perfectly well what I've seen and what I haven't. It was the same corpse with the same clothes, only today he was closer to a thicket of trees. You see, he wasn't there yesterday, but he was back again today. Very odd."

"Someone took him home for a visit?"

"Get off, Arthur. We ought to notify someone."

"I suggest you let the police handle it."

"But they haven't, they won't. This poor man, dead, all alone in the middle of a city park, and no one takes any notice. In England, when one finds a body there are procedures to follow. Here, there's nothing. What's the matter with everyone? Do you suppose it was Stalin?"

"The poor bloke in the park?"

"Don't talk wet. I mean his influence all those years and this monstrous passivity."

In a gesture he had clearly picked up from Yuri, Arthur drew down the corners of his mouth and shrugged.

18.

"Of course Arthur thinks I've gone mad," said Irene. "That is, when he bothers to think of me at all."

She and Molly had decided to walk back to the hotel from the evening rehearsal, a distance of about a mile and a half. They'd not had a chance to be off by themselves since they'd arrived in Leningrad, and Molly wanted to see how things were going, how the other actors were doing, and, in general, if there was anything, as company manager, she ought to know about. The truth was, she missed Irene.

Irene was telling Molly about the dead bodies she'd come across.

"Do you think they were suicides?" said Molly.

"Who knows? The first one might have been drunk and just rolled right into the pond. The second one is anybody's guess. What's so odd is how everyone simply takes it in stride, as if it weren't at all out of the ordinary."

"And then there was the bride, left to fend for herself," said Molly.

"As are we all, my dear, sooner or later," said Irene. "You're wise never to have married."

"Am I?" said Molly.

Irene stopped and turned to Molly.

"What I mean is, your life is so much simpler. Here I am always leaping from one screaming drama to another. Leave my third husband for a man half my age, who turns out to be a right bastard. 'My Oberon! What visions have I seen / Methought I was enamour'd of an ass.' I awaken, but do I learn my lesson? Oh no! I fling myself back into the fray, and whenever I catch sight of my darling Molly, there you are, surveying the wreckage, serene as the Buddha."

"Hardly," said Molly.

"Well, perhaps not the Buddha, but you are steady, Molly. Remarkably so."

"Maybe I should be the one to envy you."

"Don't be taken in! You're much too sensible."

"Am I?"

"Of course you are. And we'd be lost if you weren't."

They stood on an iron bridge, looking down into the slow-moving waters of a canal along a side street in the district of the Kirov. On either side were apartment buildings three or four stories high with lace curtains billowing out over the flowers in window boxes. Every once in a while, a couple would stroll by arm in arm. White nights, nearly eleven o'clock, and there hung in the air a strange, extended twilight.

Molly thought about her daydream of walking out the stage door, out of the city, through the suburbs to a meadow somewhere far away. What if there were a house there, she thought, with a lit window and a woman standing in the open doorway, waiting, her hand shielding her eyes so she could see into the distance, a woman not unlike Irene, perhaps. What if she were suddenly to turn to Irene and proclaim her love?

But she'd do nothing of the kind. She'd remain gazing at the canal and out beyond, listening to the sound of distant traffic. She'd go on being steady and reasonable because that's what was needed, what people expected of her.

"I should have joined a convent," said Molly, "but I lost the faith in junior high school. Vatican II. All of a sudden we could eat meat on Fridays. Nuns were leaving their orders to marry priests. Nothing made sense anymore. At the same time, I knew the world held nothing for me, really. I was in crisis. Then one day after school, my sophomore year, I wandered into the auditorium and followed voices I heard backstage. Kids were painting scenery for a play. The Drama Club. I picked up a brush, and that was that. I've been in the theater ever since. It became the one thing I could believe in, more honest than religion because no one ever claimed it was real. Yet it was closer to the truth, a truth I could accept: a make-believe world that mirrored a world of illusion. Less hurtful than the church by far."

Molly heard them first: finger cymbals, bells, a drum, voices chanting. When she turned, she expected to see what she'd seen from the train, the procession she'd seen in her dream. However, what she now saw approaching was a group of maybe thirty people in saffron robes, their heads shaved and lines painted on their foreheads, wagging back and forth as they half marched, half skipped up the narrow pavement leading to the bridge. Remembering her dream, Molly imagined they'd lead her to the seashore, the bride and groom standing under a silk tent. But they were Krishnas of course; she recognized them as they stepped onto the bridge, touching Irene's and Molly's shoulders, hair, and faces with their grimy hands, chanting "*Hare Rama, Rama Rama,*" beckoning them to follow. The two women stood back to let them pass, and only when they'd gone did Molly let her body relax and breathe normally again. Irene touched her shoulder to reassure her and grinned:

"Come, my lord, and in our flight
Tell me how it came this night
That I sleeping here was found
With these mortals on the ground."

She and Molly headed back toward the boulevard where taxis and streetcars collected people as they streamed out of the ballet. Farther along, they came across a crowd that had gathered around a man and woman in whiteface, wearing street clothes, performing some sort of skit. The woman screeched and beat the stout man about the face with her flattened hands. The man shouted and raised his arms to the sky. The crowd laughed. The man grabbed a handwritten sign from a nearby suitcase and held it up. The crowd laughed again. Molly and Irene stood a long time, laughing with the others, though they had no idea what the skit was about.

Then, turning back toward the hotel, Molly heard a brass band in the distance, playing something slow and mournful, a song she recognized from Soviet films, a song popular during the Great Patriotic War. And she remembered the story about Shostakovich riding his bicycle through the streets of Leningrad during the blockade, looking for enough musicians who were still alive to rehearse a new symphony. She could picture him peddling slowly, swaying from side to side, past dead bodies wrapped in rags, people foraging for wood, pale faces numbed by shock and hunger. That year, they say, even the rats disappeared because there was no food.

She wanted to tell Irene the story, but Irene looked so bemused by the skit they'd seen or some private thought, that Molly took her arm instead and, without speaking, guided her through the jostling crowd.

19.

As a young man, Yuri had risen quite fast in the KGB and had traveled with Andropov as his interpreter, even when Andropov was general secretary of the party's Central Committee. Sometime after that, however, Yuri had fallen back through the ranks, a fact he attributed to a change in administration. That's when he went to see Mikhail Sergeyevich, who hired him because he could sell military watches and belt buckles and nesting dolls in five different languages. Soon enough, Mikhail Sergeyevich recognized Yuri's intelligence and loyalty, so that he rose once again through the ranks, this time of private enterprise.

Today, however, Yuri sat outside the office of his old boss at the KGB, the assistant to the undersecretary of the general supervisor of a small district outside Leningrad. The receptionist had announced Yuri three times, and yet he still waited. A political crisis, something to do with the trouble in the Baltics, he supposed. He had no way of knowing. He flipped through an old issue of *Moscow Life*, which showed Russian women in folk costumes greeting tourists. He was scanning an article about an international parapsychology conference when the door opened and there stood Pyotr Grigorevich, his former supervisor, looking worn and drawn and sour, more nervous than usual.

"You, then," he said. "What do you want?"

Yuri stood at attention and saluted. "I have information in which, I am certain, you will take a special interest," he said.

"Come in. Be quick about it."

Pyotr Grigorevich sat at his desk. Yuri remained standing.

"I have come here today, sir, to report a crime against the State."

"Indeed." Pyotr Grigorevich lit another cigarette off the one he had left in the ashtray. Yuri noticed he didn't offer him one. "Get on with it."

"A most heinous crime. So vile," said Yuri, "it is with difficulty that I utter its name."

"I haven't got all day."

"The crime, sir, of ... sodomy."

"The culprit?"

"A foreigner, sir."

"And how do you come by your information?"

"He has approached a Soviet citizen for sexual favors."

"And has this Soviet citizen complied?"

"Yes and no."

"Yes and no?"

"Yes."

"Yes?"

"No. Not exactly. What I mean to say is, he has skillfully lured the foreigner into a trap, so the State might benefit from, shall we say, a steep fine."

"The foreigner has money."

"Sir, all foreigners have money."

"Some more than others. Why is he in the country?"

"He's an actor."

"From Hollywood?" Pyotr Grigorevich's face brightened.

"From London. He's with a small troupe of English and Americans at the invitation of the Janus Society of International Friendship and Understanding Through the Dramatic Arts."

Pyotr Grigorevich closed his eyes and blew two streams of smoke out his nose.

"Is he famous, then?"

"Not actually. I mean, not very."

"In other words, not at all. The fine wouldn't be enough to cover the cost of the paperwork, not to mention your cut. What's the matter, comrade, selling trinkets to tourists not putting food on the table?"

"Mikhail Sergeyevich has many enterprises, all of which are showing handsome profits."

"Then why bother with this foreign pederast?"

"Old loyalty," said Yuri.

"New poverty, you mean. Go ask Mikhail Sergeyevich for a rise in pay. I don't care who's poking whom out there; it's all the same to me. If you want to help your old comrades, bring us a buyer for plutonium. That's where the money is today. We can't live on bribes anymore. We've had to diversify; the competition is fierce, and with this inflation … You know as well as I. Now get out; I've got work to do."

"Yes sir," said Yuri, saluting again. Then he turned on his heel and marched out. Just as he stepped into the waiting room, the door slammed behind him. The receptionist lifted both palms skyward, smiled, and shrugged. Then she turned back to the magazine she was reading.

20.   .

"It's probably nothing," said Amanda. "A wrong number, perhaps."

She and Irene were walking through Gostiny Dvor, pretending to shop. There was nothing to buy.

"But three times in one night. Each time just as I was getting back to sleep, the phone would ring—as if he knew."

"You think it was a man."

"No way of telling. Didn't say anything. Just waited on the other end of the line and then hung up. And Arthur was out all night. I was terrified."

"Have you told anyone else?"

"No."

"Does anyone know you've met me?"

"Just Arthur, but I haven't told him why you're here, not really. Just about the joint ventures."

"And where was he last night?"

"That's just it. I don't know. With Yuri, I suspect. I'm afraid he's fallen in love."

"I see."

"What do you see?"

"It may be that someone is about to blackmail Arthur. Or someone might be trying to get at me through you."

"Good God."

"Don't worry, Irene. If you show them you're afraid—in any case, it's important to remain calm, that's all. As I say, it's probably nothing."

She took a rumpled black T-shirt from an otherwise empty shelf and held it up against Irene; it was miles too small.

"Even so," Amanda said, "it's best not to ring me. Let's arrange to meet somewhere, say, Tuesday a week."

21.

On opening night, Arthur did not, at first, realize he was playing to an empty house. The auditorium seemed quiet, unusually quiet, but he reckoned *some*one was out there. As he began his first speech, he noticed the first few rows were empty. Russians are shy, he thought. They don't like to sit in the front row, that's all. But by the time Irene had made her entrance, he could tell there was not a soul out there.

"What's the point of going on?" cried Susan backstage.

"Think of it as another dress rehearsal," said Burt.

"*No*," said Molly. "Think of it as you would any other performance. This is the real thing."

"Ridiculous," said Susan.

"I'm warning you," said Molly.

So they went on with the wedding scene, "Pirate Jenny," "The Song of Heavy Cannon," straight through to the "First Threepenny Finale." Irene, Arthur, and Susan sang:

"We take no comfort from you bunk
For everything's a heap of junk."

Arthur:

"The world is poor and men are bad
There is of course no more to add."

All three:

"We do not mind confessing
The whole thing is depressing
We take no comfort from your bunk
For everything's a heap of junk."

As act two began, Arthur whispered to Molly, "There's someone out there, standing way back under one of the exit signs. Looks to be leaning on a mop."

"Play to her as if she were the queen," said Molly.

When the curtain closed after the last act, Susan turned and started toward her dressing room in a huff, but Irene grabbed her arm.

"Not so fast, dearie," she said. "We've still got the curtain calls."

The woman at the back of the hall had taken up a slow, rhythmic clapping (Commie clapping, Burt called it), the way people applaud in Russia, but to have it issue from only one person sounded eerie and mournful, as if she were the last theatergoer applauding the last performance of the last play on Earth, the end of the whole human drama.

There she stood (God love her, thought Arthur), applauding the thieves and beggars and prostitutes, the Preacher, the Chief of Police, and the Murderer redeemed by the Queen … until the curtain closed for a final time.

Everyone broke rank and started to talk. Then Arthur shushed them. The woman at the back was calling out. He opened the curtain.

"Yes?" he said.

"*Oyay! Pazhaluystra*," she said.

Arthur called Yuri over to translate.

"She says do you want her opinion."

"Of course," said Molly, "we'd love to know what she thought."

"The music," said the old woman, "was lovely. The influence of American jazz, the voices of your singers, all render perfectly the atmosphere of Berlin in the twenties. Though that duet in the second act, those two women, really, they've got to pick up the pace. Sounds like they're running out of breath. They should quit cigarettes, maybe. I don't know, it's none of my business. On the music, you are to be commended.

"My argument," she continued, "is with your selection of the play. Thieves, prostitutes, murderers! We should come to the theater to see them? When that's all we see on our way to work, when shopping, and on our way home in the evening? Our sons and daughters, even. Which includes *you* Alexandre Nicoliavich," she said, pointing to Sasha. "*Hooligan!* You think I don't recognize you with your stage makeup? Shame on you!

"Forgive me," she said, turning back to Molly. "I know him from a little boy. His dear mother is my neighbor.

"Do you think your father," she said, turning again to Sasha, "from his place among the angels in heaven, does not see your life?"

"Wait a minute," Molly said. "Yuri. Tell her I'd like to say something."

Yuri conveyed the message.

"Certainly. Of course," said the old woman.

"What we're trying to do with this production," Molly said, "is to reflect what we see—and what Brecht saw—happening around us. What we're exploring is the possibility that the play describes life in contemporary Russia as well as life under the Communist Party, as accurately as it described life under capitalism."

"It's an old joke," the woman interrupted. "Under capitalism, man exploits his fellow man. Under Communism, it's the other way around."

"And so," said Molly, "the play has as much to say to us today as it did in 1928. This is exactly the sort of discussion we'd hoped to spark."

"Spark?" said Yuri.

"Start up. Provoke," said Molly.

"But who are *you* to criticize *us* for corruption?" shouted the old woman. "The gangster is an American invention. That's what this fellow and his hooligan friends imitate. Everything is now for sale in this country. Mothers sell their children in the Metro. Who are you to criticize what you yourself helped create—using some dead, tired piece of Marxist theater to do it?"

"But the play shows we have a choice," said Molly.

"What choice?" said the old woman. "It's a long-winded, disjointed, didactic piece of rubbish. Contradicts itself all over the place. Never did make sense."

"But it's a comedy," said Molly.

"Did you hear me laughing? Good manners is one thing, my dear; lying is another. I prefer Chekhov."

"It's not nearly as didactic as Brecht's other plays," said Molly.

"For this we can thank God," said the old woman. "The productions I've had to sit through. Torture! I'd have preferred a month in a labor camp! But I haven't made myself understood. What we need from the West is not more cynicism and despair. Yet this is all you provide."

She sang in Russian:

"What does a man live by? By resolutely
Ill-treating, beating, cheating, eating some other bloke!
A man can only live by absolutely
Forgetting he's a man like other folk!
So, gentlemen, do not be taken in:
Men live exclusively by mortal sin."

"Yuri," said Molly, "ask her how she knows the song."

"Simple," said the old woman. "In 1935 I played Polly. After the war, I played Ginny Jenny. And twenty-five years ago, I played Mrs. Peachum."

"But if you're an actress," said Molly, "what are you doing—"

"With mop and bucket? My final role. A charwoman. You've obviously never tried to live on a pension in this country—our new market economy. Can't be done. But at least it's honest work," she said, shaking her fist at Sasha, who took a step back.

The old woman rushed forward until she had almost reached the stage. She shouted at Sasha and then at Yuri. Yuri shouted back.

"What are they saying?" cried Molly.

The redheaded Russian actress stepped forward.

"They argue about the furniture," she said. "The old woman accuses us of stealing it from the flats of Widows of Decorated Veterans of the Great Patriotic War. She claims one of the widows was found murdered."

"Impossible," said Molly.

"No," said the actress, "it's not so unusual nowadays. People are often killed with no explanation or any good reason, either."

"But for props," said Irene.

"For a play in English," said Arthur.

"That no one would come to see even if it were in Russian," said Burt.

"Impossible," said Irene.

"She accuses us," continued the redheaded actress, "but you are right; it is not possible. I know Sasha. He abhors to shed the blood of human being, unless, for purpose of business, it is unavoidable. And this is not business venture, it is cultural event, and so he did not. Of this I am sure."

As suddenly as the argument had started, it stopped, and the old woman turned and walked slowly up the aisle to resume mopping the foyer.

Irene leaned over and whispered to the young Russian actress,

"Get that woman's name for me, please. I've got to talk to her."

22.

Irene threw the covers off and lunged for the phone.

"Hullo?" she said. "Hullo!"

There was someone on the other end, but no voice. Dead air. Someone moving in the background, maybe.

"Hullo!" she said.

She looked over to Arthur's bed. Still made. Hadn't been slept in. It was well after midnight.

She heard a click and then nothing.

She got a towel from the bathroom, wrapped it around the receiver twice, and left if off the hook.

Then she tried to go back to sleep.

23.

When the actors arrived at the grill-bar the next day at noon, they were met by the large blonde.

"*Nyet* lunch," she barked.

"But the agreement was for three meals a day," said Molly. "That's what we've paid for."

After Molly convinced her to let the actors eat, at least for today—they had rehearsal at two—the woman directed Molly to her supervisor's office. She pointed upward, jabbing her finger into the air. She had exhausted her English and, evidently, her goodwill. She wrote a number on a slip of paper and handed it to Molly, who went in search of the office, turning down one cavernous, toffee-colored corridor after another, following the faded path in the middle of the worn brown carpeting, up one staircase and then another, until she found 518.

She knocked. The door opened, and there stood a gigantic woman with a helmet of smooth, evenly colored auburn hair. She crossed her arms like a sultan. Molly showed her the letter she'd received from the Janus Society explaining the terms of the agreement with the hotel, but the sultan did not read English, and began a speech that grew increasingly agitated, first pointing, then waving her arm like a sword.

"May I use your phone?" said Molly, pointing to the desk.

The woman extended her right arm in silence.

"Yuri!" said Molly when he answered. "They refused to serve us lunch at the grill-bar. I'm in the supervisor's office. Could you explain to her that we're supposed to get three meals a day? Just as before. Nothing has changed. For the full six weeks. It's what we've paid for. Explain it to her. There's been some misunderstanding."

Molly handed the phone over to the sultan, who put on her glasses, opened a large ledger, and ran a bright red fingernail down a column of numbers. She shook her head. She frowned. She shouted into the phone. She glared at Molly. Molly smiled back. The woman made clucking sounds and shook her head again, more slowly this time. Then she cooed and pleaded for mercy (or so it seemed to Molly), as if she were talking to a lover. Whatever Yuri was doing, it worked, for now the woman smiled and said in Russian what Molly could only assume amounted to: "All right. I'll take care of it."

24.

That night, back at the hotel after rehearsal, there came a knock on Molly's door.

"It's Yuri," said the voice on the other side.

"What's wrong?" she said.

"Nothing," he said, "I just want to talk with you. May I?"

Molly opened the door a crack. "Can't it wait till tomorrow?"

He pulled a bottle of wine from behind his back.

"I'm exhausted, Yuri. I'm going to bed."

"Please," he said, "I want to explain. You must not have wrong impression of us."

"In the morning, Yuri."

"We Russians are complicated people. We are in a delicate situation regarding this cultural exchange and your theater company. You must understand. We have made sacrifices, sometimes at our own personal expense—"

"This will have to wait until breakfast."

"—to ensure not only your comfort but also your safety. No one could have foreseen this unfortunate occurrence. How shall I say, the mistake in understanding with your producer."

"Stop. I really mean it."

Yuri brushed his cheek against the bottle, rounding his lips a bit. "I was so hoping we could have a little drink and talk. Besides, I would like to know you better, Mollichka."

"I'll take a rain check."

Yuri looked perplexed.

"Some other time," said Molly. "I'm going to bed now. Good night."

As she closed the door, she could see Sasha backing out of Susan's room with his shoes in one hand, blowing a kiss with the other. When he saw Yuri, Sasha started toward him, but when he saw Molly, he turned on his heel and strode stiffly away down the hall.

25.

"Because, Arthur, something very odd is going on, and I intend to get to the bottom of it."

"Don't get involved," he said.

He and Irene were getting ready for bed.

"It's too important to ignore. I couldn't live with myself."

"You don't actually believe what that old woman was saying, do you?"

"Why wouldn't I?"

"She's a charwoman, Irene. She'd most likely been at the vodka."

"How many charwomen do you know who could discuss the theater the way she did?"

"I knew a woman at the Old Vic made some very astute remarks about Sir Laurence's Henry the Fifth."

"I'm taking Amanda to see her."

"That journalist friend of yours?"

"Yes."

"What's she been filling your head with?"

"She's not filling my head with anything, Arthur. She knows a great deal about Russia. In fact—Arthur, I need your help. Can you keep a secret?"

"Of course."

"Swear it."

"I swear."

"On your knees."

"Irene!"

"On your knees."

"All right. I swear. Now what is it?"

"She knows Mikhail Sergeyevich. As a matter of fact,

they're— Well, she's interviewed him. He's in the Mafia. Very important, very high up."

"If he's so important, why would he grant an interview to some English women's magazine?"

"It just so happens she's under contract to Putnam for a book on organized crime in Russia. You've sworn to never tell a living soul, remember. What's more, she's a foreign correspondent for the *Financial Times*."

"Never heard of her."

"Because all you ever read is *Variety* and the *Daily Mail*."

"Never mind. If this bloke is a gangster, why does he go round giving interviews?"

"To prove he's above the law. To show off, I suppose."

"I still say keep out of it."

"As if you were any good at that."

"What do you mean?"

"Our young friend, Yuri."

"Yes?"

"Arthur. How long have I known you?"

"Thirty years, I should think."

"Longer than your three wives put together."

"And so? What are you driving at, Irene?"

"It was clear enough on the train, your mooning at him all the time. Then sneaking out of our room at all hours, never coming home some nights. But now: kissing in the wings at rehearsal—"

"You saw."

"And who knows who else saw? What if you're caught? It's not like England, you know. A slap on the hand and a fine for cottaging. He might be setting a trap, Arthur. The phone's been ringing in the middle of the night. Two or three times. And someone's on the other end, I can tell. Amanda thinks it

might be someone getting ready to blackmail you. Yuri's got
to be in on it."

"Nonsense. He's a reformed alcoholic."

"That's why he takes you out for drinks and chats Molly up
with a bottle of wine."

Arthur looked stung. "And he's quit the KGB."

"Oh Christ, Arthur." Irene began throwing things into her
makeup bag.

"It was a job, you know. He was young."

"Arthur, you don't just quit the KGB. It's like the Catholic
Church, they've got a finger on you for life." She stood up and
began to pace.

"But everything's changed, Irene. I should think it's more like
the British Council now. Quite harmless."

"Quite. And just what did Yuri do for the KGB? Or isn't he
at liberty to say?"

"Interpreter. He traveled. Perfectly innocent."

"Innocent!" Irene shouted. "He may well have murdered an
old woman to get us our props. He's in league with them, that's
for sure. And he's most likely behind the campaign to drive me
mad by ringing me up at all hours."

Irene stormed around the room, picking up her dressing
gown, a pillow, and snatching a blanket off her bed.

"You're blind!" she screamed. "And stupid! And selfish. And
now you're going to get us all killed!"

"Irene," said Arthur.

But she was already halfway down the hall.

26.

There came another knock at Molly's door.

"Go away!" shouted Molly.

"It's Irene," said the voice on the other side.

Molly opened the door.

"Was Yuri just here with a bottle of wine?" Irene looked incensed.

"Trying to apologize for the grill-bar."

"That's the least of our worries," said Irene as Molly closed the door behind her. "Molly, you've no idea. Arthur and I have had a row. He's gone mad. Over Yuri. Who is most likely going to have us all murdered in our beds. Well, he won't find me in mine. Not tonight."

Irene dropped her blanket and pillow on the floor and threw her arms around Molly's neck. She sobbed, but not for long. In the next moment, she drew away and sat on the bed.

"What the charwoman said the other night. That's not the half of it. Oh Molly, I ought to have come to you sooner, but I was sworn to secrecy."

"Slow down," said Molly. "What's this about?"

"The Mafia. Mikhail Sergeyevich. Amanda Peters."

"Who's Amanda Peters?"

"An Englishwoman, a writer. I met her at the covered market. She's doing a book on organized crime in Russia. She knows Mikhail Sergeyevich because he's one of the local bosses. Yuri works for him. Arthur seems to be having an affair with Yuri. I'm getting anonymous phone calls at all hours of the night. And Arthur refuses to believe we're in danger. You see it's blackmail, it's got to be."

"We'll sort it out in the morning."

"Well, I'm not going back to that room. I can't."

Molly looked at Irene's blanket on the floor and then at Irene who was looking at her. Then Irene looked at her blanket on the floor.

"Right. I'll just make myself a little nest there on the floor, although I doubt I'll sleep ..." Irene looked at Molly and then at the double bed. "Or I could ... I mean, I'd just take up a sliver here on the side. Won't even roll over. Promise."

"All right. All right," said Molly. "Let's just get some sleep."

27.

There came a knock on Arthur's door. Thinking it was Irene, he opened it immediately, but it was Yuri, with a bottle of wine.

"I passed Irene carrying a blanket. Is anything wrong?"

"No. Yes. We've had a row. She's gone off to sleep in Molly's room, I expect. Come in. Come in."

Arthur could hardly believe his good fortune. He put his hand on Yuri's shoulder, but Yuri ducked away, pulled a corkscrew from his pocket, and began opening the wine.

"Glasses," he said.

"I don't really fancy a drink just now," said Arthur.

"I do," said Yuri.

"But I thought—"

"It's only red wine. Good for the blood," said Yuri.

Arthur went into the bathroom to wash out the two glasses. As Yuri poured the wine, Arthur brushed his hand against Yuri's thigh, a gesture Yuri ignored.

Some hours later, after they'd made love, Yuri smoked a cigar in bed.

"What do you know about this Englishwoman, this Amanda Peters?" he said.

"Nothing much. Except Irene is quite keen on her."

"What's her background? Why is she in this country?"

"Some sort of … Something to do with business. Joint ventures. Does a bit of writing, I think Irene said."

"Her Russian is very good."

"You've met her?"

"Mikhail Sergeyevich introduced us. What does she write about?"

"Mikhail Sergeyevich, for one. Didn't she interview him?"

"Why would she write about Mikhail Sergeyevich?"

"He's a businessman, isn't he? Some sort of article about Russian entrepreneurs, perhaps. I really couldn't say."

"Where does she stay in Leningrad?"

"Haven't a clue."

"Can she be trusted?"

"In what way?"

"Never mind."

"What are you getting at, Yuri?"

"It's not important."

"Then why is everybody so bloody suspicious? It's mad. The charwoman thinks you stole our props. Irene's convinced Mikhail Sergeyevich is a gangster. And now you're interrogating me about a woman I've never even met."

"What makes Irene think Mikhail Sergeyevich is a gangster?"

"I can't say. I promised Irene."

"This Englishwoman."

"I can't say, Yuri. Let's change the subject."

"Tell me what Irene said."

"No. I can't. It's nothing, really. I'm bored with this."

"What if I were to tell you somebody's life was in danger?"

"Whose?"

"Now it is I who cannot say. All I know is the safety of your theater company may depend on my knowing what this

Englishwoman is up to. Tell me everything you know."

"It's only Irene's madness, that's all. And I'll not tell you a thing unless you promise to sleep here with me tonight."

"You know I cannot, Arthur. We are still governed by the Soviet Code. It is not as it is in England."

"That's what Irene says."

"About what? What does she know?"

"She has this insane notion you're trying to entrap me—for blackmail or something. She even thinks you may have murdered an old lady for the Persian carpets. It's this Amanda Peters. She's been filling Irene with distorted ideas."

"That's exactly how they work."

"How who works?"

"Never mind. Continue."

"Well, it just seems to me that Amanda Peters is snooping round Leningrad, looking for gangsters to interview for some sensationalist book for which she's already under contract. No doubt she's had an advance, and so she must either find key members of the underworld or make them up."

"Exactly."

"Exactly what?"

"It is how many foreign journalists portray us in Russia now." Yuri put out his cigar in the ashtray and got up to dress. "Go to sleep," he said. "I'll let myself out."

Not long after Yuri had gone, the phone rang. When Arthur answered it, he heard dead air, a click, and then nothing.

28.

Once again, Yuri found himself waiting outside the office of his superior. But this time it was Mikhail Sergeyevich who stood in the door when it opened, and he was smiling.

"Yuri," he said. "Come in. Sit down. Would you like a cigar?"

"No sir. Thank you. I have come on official business, a confidential matter. May we close the door?"

"Of course. Of course. Sit down. Are you sure you won't have a cigar?"

"No. Thank you, you're very kind. I must get to the point. I have information in which, I am sure, you will take special interest."

"Yes?"

"Concerning a certain English lady, a Miss Peters, whom I have reason to believe is a spy."

"A spy?"

"A spy."

"For whom? What are you talking about, Yuri?"

"A book. This English lady."

"Miss Peters."

"This Miss Peters is writing a book about us, about your organization."

"She told you this?"

"No, sir. She has befriended the actress, Irene Donovan."

"So *she* has told you this?"

"Not exactly."

"Yuri. Then who has told you this?"

"This information has come to me from her friend, Arthur, one of the actors."

"A friend of Miss Peters?"

"No, sir, a friend of Irene Donovan."

"I see."

"But he is most reliable, very intimate with Miss Donovan; they share a room. Miss Peters, he says, has given Miss Donovan the impression we are criminals—thieves, murderers."

"Amanda?"

"Miss Peters."

"Miss Peters, yes. Thank you, Yuri. I'll look into it. Is that all?"

Yuri coughed; something had caught in his throat. He had expected a plan to unfold, a plan to stop Miss Peters, a plan that would include him. But no. Mikhail Sergeyevich said he'd look into it. And maybe nothing would happen. Nothing at all.

"Yes, sir," said Yuri, turning to go. Then he turned back. "Are you sure you wouldn't like me to … I mean, I could, perhaps—"

"No, Yuri. That's quite all right. You've done very well. I'll take care of it from this point on."

"Yes, sir," said Yuri and left the office.

29.

After rehearsal the next morning, Irene headed straight for the hotel grill-bar for lunch. Such as it was: a small pot of yesterday's soup, a stale slice of black bread, a piece of gristly meat, and a small lump of egg or fish salad made with rancid-smelling mayonnaise.

"They're trying to poison us," said Burt.

"What did we do wrong?" cried Lil, who loved to eat. "They were so nice in the beginning."

"*Some*one," said Susan, "must have offended them. They're very sensitive, you know." She was chewing on a piece of black bread. "Soulful," she said.

"Oh, never mind," said Irene. "I wasn't really all that hungry." She was supposed to meet Amanda Peters in front of the Dom Knigi in an hour and a half, and she wanted to give herself enough time to walk, a good forty minutes. She didn't trust a taxi.

She raised her head and looked toward the bar. "*Koffia pazhalusta.*"

The two waitresses sat together at a table underneath the television and stared up into the blue light. They were both smoking. Evidently they hadn't heard, so Irene walked up to the bar and waited for them to notice her. The television showed policemen hauling a body out of an apartment, then another body slumped in a stairwell, then a table full of confiscated firearms.

Irene cleared her throat.

"I—I beg your par—" she began. "*Pazhalusta*," she said. "*Esch koffia?*"

Without looking away from the screen, the older of the two women said, "*Nyet koffia.*"

"*Nyet koffia?*" said Irene. "But how is that possible? Surely there's coffee. *Poocheemoo?*"

"*Kofevarka*," said the woman, pointing to the machine. Irene reckoned it was broken.

"Well, then," said Irene, "how about tea. *Esch chai?*"

"*Chai esch*," sighed the woman, heaving herself up from the table.

"*Spaseeba*," said Irene. "*Spaseebe bolshoi.*"

Brian was pushing his plate away when she got back to the table. "I can't eat this," he said.

Lil looked longingly at Brian's plate; she'd already finished what was on her own.

"I'll have Yuri talk to the staff again," said Molly. She wondered where he was.

"Maybe it's because we're not tipping," said Burt.

"Not paying is more like it," said Molly. "Yuri explained the whole thing to me, finally. The grill-bar supervisor showed him the books. All she's received is the deposit to hold the rooms. I wired Hal to find out what went wrong and asked him to send more money."

She took a telegram out of her shirt pocket, unfolded it, and showed it to Irene, who read it aloud: "Must be some mistake. Stop. All paid up. Stop. Good luck. Stop. Hal."

"What's that supposed to mean?" said Brian.

"Our producer has left us stranded," said Irene, folding the telegram and placing it on the table. "It happens. Could be worse. Could be war, a revolution. I remember some years ago in London, a troupe of Zulus—"

Irene was interrupted by the sound of the large blond woman rapping her knuckle against the bar.

"*Chai!*" shouted the woman and went back to her place in front of the television.

Irene went up to fetch her tea.

"So we're stranded here? With no money?" said Susan. "What are we going to do?"

"Keep on as we have been," said Irene as she sat down again, "until Molly tells us otherwise."

"We'll be fine," said Molly. "There are just some details to work out. Staying focused on tonight's performance is what counts. I'll keep you posted."

Molly looked tired. Of course, she probably hadn't slept. Irene had tossed and turned all night, despite her promises. She must make it up to Molly, who was, as always, being uncommonly brave. Did she know? Had anyone told her? More than bravery, it was also her genius for listening for what was actually happening, beneath whatever appeared to be going on. In rehearsal, in one's life.

This was as natural to Molly as breathing, one barely noticed it at all, yet they gathered themselves, these moments with Molly, and became part of one's being. Now, still looking at Molly, Irene felt no one had ever listened as well, not her husbands, not her lovers, not even her own mother.

Irene turned her head. Susan had asked her a question.

Molly felt her heart sear and wither. Susan asked some stupid question to divert Irene's attention, just as Molly had felt herself on the verge of receiving some precious gift from Irene. And Susan had snatched it away. ("Irene, that perfume you're wearing, did you buy it here?") So she would never know what it was. She would excuse herself, go up to her room and take a nap. She hadn't slept, and tonight was the performance for their sponsors, Mikhail Sergeyevich and his men. But she couldn't move. She felt herself sink. She sat up straight, took a deep breath. She would talk, then, struggle back to the surface and be carried along by conversation, something Burt was saying he'd heard from Sasha, that Russia was like two men wrestling in a dense fog at the edge of a cliff.

But what did it matter? Comparing one thing to another. What difference did it make? She had glimpsed a gift that had been snatched away. And yet something had passed between Molly and Irene, had risen for a moment like a cloth lifted by wind, a silk tent billowing above their heads.

30.

She noticed the shoes first. She was crossing Fontanka, on her way to Dom Knigi. Two men were standing over the body on a steep, grassy slope. Women's shoes. Well made. Stylish in a way Russian shoes were not.

Irene ran across the bridge and found her way to the slope. She noticed a rope around the neck of the body. The body lay facedown. The men were turning her over. Her clothes were dry. She'd hung herself. The men covered her with a blanket. Hung herself. Or been hung. Irene knew those shoes, and before she even realized that she'd begun to scream, one of the men had his hand over her mouth, shushing her. Trying to calm her down. That was it. Not killing her. Then the second man was by her side, repeating something in Russian that sounded like a prayer.

She couldn't breathe. She gasped, and the man let her go. Irene coughed and began to wail softly to herself. Rocking back and forth slowly, she pulled up clumps of grass and let them go. Though she was at some distance from the body and hadn't really seen the face, she knew it was Amanda. A blue scarf. A small spiral notebook. Familiar things. English things.

While the men were struggling to get the body back up the slope to street level, Irene grabbed the notebook in one hand, her pocketbook in the other, and ran.

By the time she got back to the hotel, she had imagined several different stories that resulted in the scene she'd come upon. That Amanda Peters had been executed by gangsters was never in doubt. When Irene finished the second of four bottles of Georgian wine Arthur had bought as gifts for people back home, she stood staring out the window at the pale yellow wall across the street. She would confront Yuri. No. She would call the British embassy, get someone there to help her. No. Better go there herself; the phones were tapped. She'd check all the morgues. She felt she'd been a fool to leave the body, but there's no telling what might have happened to her if she'd stayed.

The notebook was blank. Amanda hadn't even had a chance to write in it. But where were her other notes, the notes for her book? Her apartment. Where had she lived? And how to get in? She would tell Molly, but she needed a Russian, a Russian she could trust. The old woman who cleaned the theater. She'd know what to do. Irene put another bottle of wine in her large bag and set out for the theater. She was late.

31.

"Where's Irene?" asked Molly.

"Dunno. Haven't seen her," said Arthur. "Not in her dressing room?"

"No, and it's ten minutes till curtain. She wasn't in your room at the hotel?"

"I didn't go up. Stopped for a sandwich in the grill-bar and came here straightaway."

"This isn't like her, Arthur. And on the one night we have an audience."

"Nearly a full house. Our esteemed sponsors. I should think half of Leningrad's underground is in this evening—under threat of death."

"Yuri," called Molly. "Find the woman who was here opening night, the woman who cleans the theater."

"You can't be thinking—" said Arthur.

"Why not?" said Molly. "She's played Mrs. Peachum before; I'm bringing her out of retirement."

"She doesn't understand a word of English, even if she remembers the part. It was years ago."

"We'll go by the beats. She can do it in Russian, timing herself to the speeches around her. And we'll hope for the best."

Yuri arrived with Maria Ivanovna.

"Ask her if she'd do us a favor," said Molly.

Yuri began to translate, and the old woman waved him away. "I understand a little of English," she said.

"Something's happened," said Molly. "Something's happened to Miss Donovan, the actress who plays Mrs. Peachum. Could you go on for her?"

"Of course," said Maria Ivanovna. "Dress me. Tell me what to do." She unbuttoned her blouse, while Molly opened the script.

"I will say my lines in Russian. Yes?" she said. "I have enough of English perhaps to know where to speak, but not enough of English to say the lines. I don't remember exactly the words in Russian, but I can say what comes close. I shall signal to the next person to speak by nod my head as I finish, yes?"

"Wonderful," said Molly. "Thank you. Susan, Arthur, Burt, Lil, Brian? Did you get that? Look for Mrs. Peachum to nod at the end of her speeches. That's your cue. Stay on top of it. Yuri, tell the Russian actors."

The one-armed actor held a mirror while the redheaded actress helped Maria with her makeup.

"Now, Miss Ivanovna," said Molly, "if you get lost, look down. I'll be in the prompter's box. Let's just hope for the best. I can't thank you enough for doing this."

"Wait until after. It could be a disaster," Maria Ivanovna said.

The overture began, the curtain rose: beggars begged, thieves thieved, whores whored, and the balladeer sang "The Ballad of Mack the Knife."

When Maria Ivanovna stepped onstage, a roar went up from the stalls. At first Molly thought there was trouble, but when she peered out of the prompter's box and saw Mikhail Sergeyevich standing with everyone else, she realized they were cheering. They all knew who she was.

Maria Ivanovna took a deep bow.

Molly held her breath when it came time for Maria Ivanovna's first speech, and didn't exhale again until the quick exchange with Arthur, which was actually getting laughs. When they managed to stay on beat during their duet and ended on the last note together, Molly began to think everything was going to go smoothly.

So smoothly, in fact, she'd almost forgotten about Irene until she heard muffled voices coming from backstage.

32.

Irene had snuck in quietly through the stage door and taken Yuri's pistol from his jacket pocket. Then she knocked over a metal chair in the dark and it clattered to the floor. She winced when she saw Arthur step toward her. His face was all screwed up, and he was shushing. He wanted to keep her from what she'd come to do. She knew that. No trouble. For God's sake don't make trouble. That was Arthur all over. That's what was wrong with him, in fact, and she must remember to tell him, but first she stepped forward to push him out of the way. Instead, she fell into his arms and started to cry.

"Are you all right, darling?" he whispered.

"No," Irene said through her sobs.

"But what is it?" whispered Arthur.

"I haven't time to explain," said Irene, steadying herself.

"Irene," said Arthur, "you're drunk."

"Of course I am. If only you knew." She grabbed his shirt and pulled him close. "But there's no time. I've got to kill Mikhail Sergeyevich," she whispered.

"You're mad," said Arthur.

Irene smiled and fluttered her eyelids.

"But who's playing me?" she asked, peering through the scrim.

33.

Mikhail Sergeyevich hadn't enjoyed himself at the theater so much in years. He roared with laughter and pinched the arm of the young lady seated next to him.

"You don't see that every day, now, do you?"

His companion found the whole thing unsettling. She didn't like it that the Russian women, many of whom she knew, were portraying whores. She didn't know what the play was about, but she suspected the Russians were going to be made to look ridiculous in the end.

She slapped Mikhail Sergeyevich's hand and wiggled in her tight evening gown. She didn't know who this famous old woman was, the only one speaking Russian, or why her boyfriend was so taken with her. The English actors argued onstage, and though she didn't understand the words, the tone was unmistakable.

> POLLY: "You—shut your filthy mouth, you slut, or I'll give you a smack in the chops, dear Miss!"
>
> LUCY: "I'll have you kicked out, Miss Insolence! It's no use mincing words with you. You don't understand delicacy."
>
> POLLY: "You and your delicacy! I'm compromising my own dignity! And I'm too proud for that … I am!" (*She weeps loudly.*)
>
> LUCY: "Well, look at my stomach, you trollop! Aren't your eyes open yet?"
>
> POLLY: "Oh! That! I suppose you're hoping to make something out of it? You should never have let yourself in for

it, you fine lady!"

MACHEATH: "Polly!"

POLLY: (*sobbing*) "This is really too much, Mac, this shouldn't have happened. I just don't know what I shall do!"

Instead of Maria Ivanovna as Mrs. Peachum, it was Irene who entered, wearing street clothes and carrying Yuri's pistol. "Stop!" she cried.

"I quit," said Susan. "Come on, Sasha, let's get out of here."

"You'll do nothing of the kind," said Irene, aiming the gun at Susan. "It's unprofessional." In a louder voice, she spoke her lines: "*I knew it. She's with her fancy man. Come here this minute, you filthy trollop … A fine way to behave to your poor old mother.*"

"Unprofessional!" rasped Susan. "You stagger in here blind drunk in the middle of act two, and you talk about professionalism? *Leave me alone, Mama, you don't know*—" she shouted.

"*I'll tell you what I don't know*," said Irene. Then she suddenly remembered what she had come to do and turned to face the back of the stage, for it was all lit up. She took aim.

"Mikhail Sergeyevich! I accuse you of the murder of my friend and fellow countrywoman Amanda Peters."

Arthur put his hands on her shoulders.

"Don't try to stop me!" she cried.

"You're facing the wrong way," he said.

She turned around and squinted. She raised the pistol. Those in the audience who hadn't ducked behind their seats now lay on their stomachs, weapons drawn on Irene.

Mikhail Sergeyevich ordered his men to hold their fire.

"I must try to understand you," he said. "Miss Peters is— dead? But how? And—why?" He leaned against the back of an aisle seat.

"Don't pretend you know nothing about it," shouted Irene. "You run the whole show!"

"Miss Donovan, I assure you. I have not heard— If you only knew. You see, I loved—I am—"

"Speed it up, fat boy," said Irene. She now held the gun with both hands; she'd begun to sway.

"I have no reason to murder a woman like Miss Peters. I will find the murderer and bring him to justice. I assure you."

"Gangster justice? What good is that, Mr. Bofio Mossiosa."

"Irene!" A woman's voice came from the back of the theater. "Put the gun down."

Irene shaded her eyes with one hand. Mikhail Sergeyevich turned. As she walked down the center aisle, they could see it was Amanda Peters.

"He's right," she said. "There's been some mistake."

"Risen from the dead," said Susan with a smirk.

"Imagine!" said Burt. "We could have been doing tent revivals all along."

"We'd have made a fortune," said Lil.

"Oh, do shut up!" said Irene. The arm holding the gun had gone limp and now dangled at her side. She rubbed her head with her other hand. "But your shoes; they were English shoes. And your blue scarf from Liberty's. And the little notebook."

"Irene," said Amanda. "Look at me. I'm alive. It was somebody else you saw."

Arthur caught Irene as she slumped to the floor.

Mikhail Sergeyevich leaped onto the stage, calling for a damp cloth and vodka. He knelt down and gathered Irene's limp body toward him. Arthur, who hadn't really got a proper grip on her, stood up, and Maria Ivanovna knelt down on the other side of Irene to take his place. At first Molly thought she was going to wrest Irene's body from the clutches of Mikhail Sergeyevich, but she began stroking Irene's hair and started to sing. Softly. A lullaby, Molly supposed. Mikhail Sergeyevich joined in, then Sasha and the redheaded actress, and then the others. One by one, the gangsters and the women in the audience approached the stage—singing.

34.

Molly stood in her prompter's box. Maria Ivanovna pressed her round face, beaming like the moon, against Irene's cheek. Mikhail Sergeyevich smoothed Irene's hair and sang in his deep voice a song so aching and slow, Molly might have known it all her life. She stood still and watched.

They continued to revive Irene slowly, gently, so she wouldn't be startled by the faces around her onstage. The thieves and beggars, the sheriff, the prostitutes, all started to murmur when Irene finally opened her eyes. She stirred and was about to speak, but then lay back again and smiled, gave herself in perfect faith to those who held her, the way she gave herself to everything, despite heartbreak and betrayal, because it never occurred to Irene not to give herself.

Molly climbed out of the prompter's box and onto the stage. Irene smiled and reached out her hand.

"Can you ever forgive me?" she said.

"Never mind," said Molly, letting Irene's hand rest in her own. She reached through the others to touch Irene's face, but just as she did, Irene turned to look at Maria Ivanovna.

Never mind, thought Molly. There ought to have been something to say, something more than "never mind," yet whatever it was, it lay in the heart, hidden from view, deep in the mountain like a vein of gold. Something, she now felt sure, that must be very much like love.

In This Economy

1.

"You don't want anything to excite them in here," she says, "so it's strictly grays, steel grays, cold." She herself wears mauves, teal blue, a black silk blazer. They stand holding drinks in a maximum-security pod of the new prison the night before it's to be dedicated. The cocktail napkins have the name of the place printed on them in a circle, so it's hard to see where the name ends and begins. The woman speaking is a designer. She's explaining the decor.

"But you'll notice as you get into the jail area, the more minimum-security pods, there's a progression toward warmer grays, tones that read more brown—in the common areas, that is. Where they sleep, I've put them in gray monotones; there's no character to the place where they sleep. It's to keep people from being crazy."

She describes the dayroom, the Santa Fe colors she's chosen for the floor, the burgundy chairs, the greens she's carried through in the checkerboard vinyl tile in prerelease. Seafoam, with a touch of blue. Colors that calm people and at the same time depict the outside, the world of nature, where they'll be going once they're out of jail.

"No exposed anything," she says, "standard prison design,

lighting fixtures that can't be ripped from the wall and used as weapons. Nothing sharp that can slash throats or wrists. No loose wires for strangulation."

Jack excuses himself before dinner inside the prison. He's just not up to the lobster bisque, steak, and cherries jubilee. He pleads illness and knows Trevor will make him pay later for his absence. But he has grown short of breath, listening to the designer.

She didn't start out designing prisons, she explains. She's a painter, MFA, Yale 1987.

2.

Jack smiles but shows no teeth. A prison dedication is a solemn affair. Or so he imagines. This is his first. He stands next to Trevor on a platform festooned with red, white, and blue bunting. The hot sun makes Jack blink; he's forgotten his sunglasses. His head throbs. He looks out over the schoolchildren, their shoulders flung back at attention, while a brass band plays the national anthem so loud he can't hear the children singing. Surely they *are* singing, he thinks, maybe in prepubescent voices, too high to register against the brass. He squints to see if their little mouths are moving. In school, when the music teacher told him not to sing because he was pulling everyone else off pitch, he used to mouth the words, which makes him think of the goldfish his brother had as a kid. It would open and close its mouth, as if it were saying "Yup … yup." That's how it breathed.

The prison is named for Trevor's uncle Bob, his American uncle, and Jack's head is splitting because he's back in the habit of having a few brandies after dinner. It's actually the prerelease unit that's named for Uncle Bob; the prison bears the county's name, the name of a tribe of Indians, seven syllables, impossible to pronounce.

Uncle Bob was Trevor's favorite. One of them. He has several favorite uncles, all rich, each one generous and very fond of Trevor. Sometimes Jack imagines Trevor springing fully formed from the head of one of these uncles, for Trevor never talks about his parents, though he must have had them. But he was raised, for reasons Jack will never understand, by all these uncles, and now that Bob is dead, Trevor stands to inherit yet another fortune. That's why they're here.

The governor is praising Uncle Bob and this new prison, which is state-of-the-art electronic, knows when to open and close its doors and for whom, will remember everything about each one of its inmates and guards, even the visitors. It will create new jobs for the region, which, to Jack, seems largely uninhabited.

They've come here from Europe—Belgium or France. Jack's not really sure which; they've been traveling so much. A French-speaking country, of that much he's certain, and not Africa. He's not clear about where they go from here. Vancouver or San Francisco, he thinks, depending upon whom Trevor wants to visit next. He seems to be showing Jack to all his friends, and he has friends all over the world.

Jack doesn't allow himself to wonder what will happen when they've finished the tour.

The governor has stopped speaking. Trevor is next. He thanks the governor, the architect, the wardens, the schoolchildren, a number of whom have begun pushing and pinching one another. Jack loses the thread of what Trevor is saying. The sun, this headache—he concentrates on Trevor's smile, not too broad, just right. Trevor lifts the oversized scissors to cut the ribbon.

Drivers start the engines of the blue vans full of prisoners, and as they roll toward the gate, Jack feels a line of sweat begin its course down his back, between his shoulder blades.

3.

The hotel room is beige. Everything is a slightly lighter or darker version of this color. Jack wonders if the prison decorator would say this is moving toward or away from nature and life on the outside. "There's no character to the place where they sleep," she'd said. "It's to keep people from being crazy."

He is lying down, trying to take a nap, but he's fully awake, listening to the soft, mechanical ssshhhhh of the air conditioner that cools or warms as necessary and removes all odors from the room, except the faint scent of disinfectant and what may be strawberry air freshener. The room is too cold, or too warm. He's given up fiddling with the knobs.

Too beige, perhaps. It hurts him.

He turns and stares at the curtains, which don't seem to be made of cloth. He's trying to decide what other color is in it, this beige. Does it cool to blue, or warm toward brown? Nothing is quite white.

He sneezes, imagines the droplets sucked into the machine under the window, dried, filtered, the germless air shot up the vents and released into the sky. Jack often catches cold in air conditioning, yet he wonders how anyone can get sick in this country; it's so clean, this air, no odor, everything steril-ized, contagion banished. Even so, in these rooms friends and strangers alike transmit microscopic organisms, viruses, crab lice. How betrayed they must feel, itching and scratching in all this sanitation.

Jack turns onto his other side, faces the bed opposite: flat, smooth, empty. And this is what he wants for himself today. No acid stomach, no throbbing head.

Flat, smooth, empty.

Beige.

When he does sleep, he dreams of mixing paint to achieve this beige: a small mound of burnt umber, a pile of white, some yellow ocher, perhaps, but he can't duplicate it. When he applies the paint to canvas, it contains deep reds, purples, flashes of green and gold, so he wipes the paint off with a rag dipped in solvent and begins again.

4.

Once, in Boston, they are getting ready for a garden party held each year after Harvard's graduation. Jack and Trevor have just begun their travels together and have come to Boston from Russia. It is only six or seven months after the crash on Wall Street, and Jack's paintings are next to worthless. He's lost all the money he's invested in real estate, and Trevor has saved him from the grim possibility of teaching in Yale's MFA program.

Jack is just putting on a red-and-white striped blazer when Trevor comes out of the bathroom, stops short.

"You're not wearing *that*," he says.

"Why not?" asks Jack.

"This is Cambridge," says Trevor. "*Har*vard. You're the American. You should know better."

So Jack fetches a lightweight tan jacket and gray slacks from his suitcase.

"Much better," says Trevor.

5.

They are in Santa Fe for Christmas one year. Accompanying them at a small table are a punkish blond with a nose ring; his lover, an older Finn with snakeskin boots; and a German wearing a full-length fur coat and a white ten-gallon hat. They have been drinking for the better part of the afternoon, trying to decide what to do—ski? shop? The German orders another round.

He turns to Jack. "Now I remember. The Biennale, Venice, a couple of years ago. Your work was hot. What are you doing now?"

"Traveling," says Jack.

"Do you speak Churman?" the Finn asks Trevor.

"*Er ist verrückt,*" says Trevor, rolling his eyes and pointing to the kid with spiked hair, "*aus den Fremden, denn nicht Einen kenn ich, Herr, und mir und mir ein Ding su machen,*" Trevor continues, quoting a poem, Jack figures, recognizing the words "strangers," "Lord," "from me, from me."

"*Ich liebe dich,*" says Trevor, gazing at no one.

Of whom is he thinking, Jack wonders. Whom does he love?

"*Ich habe genug gehabt,*" says Trevor.

He gets up and heads out the door without another word. Some feeling floods Jack's chest, something like admiration. He imagines Trevor walking out past the edge of town and into the desert, alone. When Trevor returns to their room that night, he doesn't say where he's been. Jack doesn't ask.

6.

Trevor doesn't mind Jack drinking brandy after supper. He says it makes Jack more amusing, and Jack knows that's his job, to be amusing, a bit naughty, wry. Quiet and out of the way mostly, but ready with a good line.

Jack is supposed to remain plain American, not too rough or vulgar, but not too rarefied, either. That was the problem with Trevor's last traveling companion: He got too precious. And then too old, Jack guesses, though Jack himself is no kid. He's close to middle age, but still boyish.

Trevor seems intent on seeing the whole world, and not just the nice parts, though they rise above the dirt and the begging and the wars. They pass through, unscathed. Jack knows it's the money that lends them this immunity. More than once they've found themselves in a city under siege in the last hotel left standing, the bar full of the international press corps.

Once, in Beirut, with bombs going off everywhere, even the brandy fails to make Jack amusing. He is so scared he doesn't know what he's saying, not that it seems to matter; the natives are oblivious. They have to be out of their minds to be staying on, and yet there they sit at dinner parties, making small talk around a long table covered with white linen. When a fig tree explodes in the garden next door, everyone ducks under the table for a few minutes before the servants bring in the sorbet.

That night Jack wakes up screaming, and Trevor rocks him back and forth.

Another night, during an air raid in Sarajevo, Jack notices that sex with Trevor has never been better. For a moment he thinks he understands Trevor's predilection for anonymous sex in public places.

The danger of it.

Jack rarely thinks of what he'd do if Trevor left him by the roadside in, say, Kashmir. He is largely indifferent to the fear of being replaced. He has nothing like a contingency plan. He wonders, now, what it would be like to let go, to sink below the bottom, into the smells and noises of the world. Suddenly he longs for squalor.

Anything but the beige of this hotel room.

7.

It comes up in conversation over cocktails with the prison decorator.

"I don't know," says Jack. "I've been thinking I'd like to paint again."

"This is the first I've heard about it," says Trevor. "You haven't painted in months."

"I know. I've just been thinking. I might rent a studio."

The decorator says she knows of one Jack may be able to have for a month.

"Go to all that trouble?" says Trevor. "I'll buy you a sketchbook, and you can draw."

Trevor seems jealous, and this deepens Jack's desire to paint again.

Sometimes, when he closes his eyes, Jack sees these new paintings: two maroon bars on a red field; black ovoid shapes bleeding into yellow. He sees himself scraping away the first layer and then painting another, which he wipes off the next day, curious to see what remains of the underpainting.

He longs to press the palette knife into pigment again, is desperate to see a color he hadn't bargained for emerge from under the brush at the end of a stroke. He wants to draw from the figure: the knees, the shoulder, the eccentric toes; all the places where the body is joined to itself.

Words appeared in his old work. The letters were compositional elements; they didn't have meaning. TIDE. LUST. SLUT. Now he wants them to have meaning.

But if Jack has something to do all day, somewhere to go besides luncheons and suppers and cocktail parties, it will make Trevor look idle. And that's one of the rules. He must be as useless as Trevor. Now he feels it to be his most urgent hunger, to paint again, and yet if he follows this desire, it will throw the whole thing off-balance; it will put his present life at risk.

8.

Months earlier, at a reception in Zurich, Jack hears himself tell a story about something that happened to them in Italy. Everyone is laughing, but suddenly Jack can't remember the punch line, or even where the story is headed. He shifts attention away from himself by nodding to a blond woman wearing a large emerald ring.

"But you were at Como last season yourself," he says. "You must have run into the same thing."

"No," says the woman, laughing. "Our troubles were entirely with the *paparazzi*. One night ..."

Jack takes this opportunity to watch Trevor. Jack pretends they've never met and examines this trim, exquisitely dressed man with new interest. He notices the gray hair at his temples. He wonders if he might be falling in love.

9.

When they aren't at a dinner party, when they're in a restaurant by themselves, they eat in silence, like old married people.

Sometimes Jack hears someone at another table purring, flirting. He hears him laugh a big, theatrical laugh which shows his dinner partner and everyone else within earshot that he is having a marvelous time.

One night, someone at another table raises his voice, "I will not be quiet!" The man is close to tears.

Everything stops: conversations, the scrape of cutlery on china, the ping of crystal. Jack is struck by the depth of silence in the small, dreadfully smart restaurant in London's West End.

"I don't care who hears me!"

The shouting man rises. He throws his serviette onto the table, knocking over a water goblet. Jack notices a slight trill of envy in his spine. Trevor will think Jack is blushing from embarrassment, not delight. That is, if Trevor thinks anything at all. Trevor casts a sidelong glance toward the offending table and goes on eating. He doesn't have to say what he's thinking. Jack lifts his eyes and shrugs to give assent, as if to say: Honestly, some people. In this way, he takes his place beside Trevor, who is above this sort of behavior. Secretly, Jack wishes he and Trevor could stand up, fight with each other, grow red in the face.

But feeling, deep feeling of any kind, would ruin everything. So they sit in silence, easy enough once the disagreeable couple leaves, but it's stretched tight, this silence. They barely look at each other. They chew. They move their knives once, twice into the medallions of beef and tear away a piece small enough to lift to the mouth. Jack has learned to eat in the European way, with his left hand, prongs of the fork always down, knife in the right hand, scooping, guiding.

10.

In their five-star hotel in Moscow, there's been nothing to eat in four days. A problem with trucks, no petrol, they are told. Trouble in the Baltics. An unfortunate occurrence. At breakfast on the fifth day, one single hard-boiled egg appears on each plate with a sprig of parsley.

Not two weeks later, at the Harvard garden party, Jack sees more finger food on silver trays than he's seen in Russian shops for a month. He scans the crowd on the lawn from a raised brick patio and notices Soviet Foreign Minister Eduard Shevardnadze having a spirited talk with Julia Child via a translator.

Swapping recipes, Jack imagines.

11.

They arrive late to a party in Paris after an opening somewhere or cocktails at the embassy. They are both a little drunk. Arab men sit on the floor, singing wild songs. Jack stands, transfixed by the music. He sways with his eyes closed.

"What's that din?" says Trevor.

"Qawali music," says the cultural attaché.

"Dreadful," says Trevor.

"I quite like it," says the man from the British Council.

"Are you all right?" shouts Trevor.

Jack nods, goes on swaying.

"Are they drunk?" Trevor yells.

"Not in the usual way," says the man from the British Council.

"They ought to quiet down," says Trevor. "Somebody's likely to call the police."

Without opening his eyes, Jack leans toward Trevor. "But

this is the sixteenth arrondissement; no one gets arrested in the *seizième*."

Which becomes the joke all over Paris. For weeks the story is told, until just the punch line survives: No one gets arrested in the *seizième*.

12.

They sit naked on a small couch in their suite of rooms high above Hong Kong. Jack leans back into Trevor, dozing after sex. He reaches up, strokes Trevor's face. He wonders what Trevor is thinking but hesitates to ask, afraid of some flip remark. So he weaves what he imagines to be Trevor's thoughts into his own, reading each breath and small movement.

It's this matching thought to thought, this breathing together, their faces close—it's this high silence that makes Jack venture to believe he knows what love is. Not the fiery pulse, nor the competent moves. It's this after, the safety of it—not wit, no words at all—which allows Jack to fashion Trevor's gratitude, perhaps, the solid ground of his feeling for Jack (or is it simply fatigue?), the feeling Jack grafts onto his own.

As his eyes close, Jack sees a flowering branch—a sign, certainly, but of what? And then, his vision full of blooms, he drops, sighing, into sleep.

13.

Jack walks in a park by Lake Geneva while Trevor takes a nap back at the hotel. A damp wind blows the last leaves off the trees. A man who looks to be in his late fifties walks a small white dog, a breed Jack doesn't recognize. The man wears a dark trench coat with its collar turned up. They come to a stop together and stand side by side, looking down, then out across the water. The older man breaks the silence.

"You are American, yes?"

"Yes," says Jack. He figures it's the cut of his raincoat, which he bought in New York.

"From which place?" says the older man.

"Cleveland, originally. Cleveland, Ohio. My father was a fireman."

"A *fire*man from *Cleve*land, O*hi*o," says the older man, as if he were scanning a line of poetry.

"What kind of dog is that?" asks Jack.

"A Volpino Italiano; it's my wife's. She's living with me again. She had a stroke, and it frightened her young lover off. Your generation is squeamish, I think. No? Am I not right?"

Jack shrugs.

"You have children?"

"No," says Jack.

"My wife is younger than I. My first wife, my only wife actually. We were never divorced, even when she left me for a new young man, and I took a mistress—without much enthusiasm, I must confess, but one must do something. It's pride, really, isn't it? We men act out of a stupid pride. The truth is, I didn't want to live without a woman. Why should I? I'm not a priest; I'm not even a very good Catholic. So it's not out of duty I took my wife back into my home. It was that I fell in love with her all over again. Can you understand? She could not speak or walk or get herself to the toilet. Her mouth hung open, and she drooled. She had involuntary movements. She would hit and kick without purpose, but not, I believe, without feeling.

"She was at work one day and felt ill, so she sat down, and

the next thing she knew, she had violent diarrhea and vomiting. Her secretary took her to hospital where they said it was influenza and sent her home. She lay in her bed and thought that is that, but in the night when she got up, she—what is the word—collapsed, yes?"

"Yes."

"And so her young lover took her again to hospital, and this time they saw it was a stroke. Suddenly she was old, and the boy she shared her bed with was frightened and ashamed of himself that he wanted to leave, ashamed that he no longer had any feeling for her. So I took him aside and relieved him of his obligation. He promised to visit. That's the last we saw of him.

"For days I sat by my wife's bed, holding a hand that would all of a sudden lift out of my own as if it were going to fly away from her body and accomplish some task on the other side of the city. It was hard, at first, to know whether or not she was conscious. While I held her hand, I told her everything I remembered about our marriage, our courtship, her girlhood and family, my military service, our children—everything we had lived, all the stories we had told each other again and again in our years together.

"She opened her eyes fourteen hours later and smiled at me with half her mouth. I laughed at her. And I wept because I knew I was in love with her again, and I believed she was in love with me as well. So in the next weeks, I tried to explain the disappearance of her gigolo. Women have their pride, too, you know. Then I had to get my mistress used to the idea my wife would be living with us, and we'd both be caring for her. We fixed a room on the ground floor, and now, my mistress and I, each day, help my wife back into this life from wherever it is she has been.

"You're not married?"

"No," says Jack.

14.

They stroll down a street in Vienna, Jack and Trevor, a broad avenue with large trees in a residential neighborhood—at street level, an occasional bakery or greengrocer among the expensive shops. A well-dressed man walks his dog; he carries a little plastic bag of shit in one hand as if it were an evening bag full of pearls.

Jack draws his breath in sharply, looks to see if Trevor has seen the dead pigeon lying on the pavement ahead. The pigeon's neck curls back, its beak open. The feathers are smooth and gray, but the breast is blown open, as if from the inside. A thin bone gleams white. Around it, torn flesh and a red hollowing into the chest cavity. The wings intact. Jack wonders how it died. Unlikely it was shot, not in this neighborhood. An animal? But the wound is so specific, precise, as though something had sucked the bird's heart out.

Too late. Trevor has already seen; his face pales. Jack steps ahead to move the pigeon aside with his foot. Trevor stops, stares at the bird, turns, steps to the curb, and vomits once, soiling neither his suit nor his carefully shined shoes. He straightens, draws a handkerchief out of his pants pocket, wipes his mouth, swallows, and walks on, his head turned to study the eighteenth-century granite façades of the buildings across the street. He looks up at the tall thin windows of the upper stories.

Jack quickens his step to catch up, thinks: If only we could stop.

But that's why they keep moving. So they will never find out.

15.

When he does sleep, Jack dreams of a prison uprising. He's in a room he shares with Trevor, like a dormitory room at college. His brother's goldfish swims in a brandy snifter on the table. The inmates have taken over everything. It's the evening of the second day. Trevor goes out to see what's happening. Jack feels as if he's hiding, yet all the other men know where he is. He's afraid, but there seems to be no danger. Jack knows the prisoners have made demands, but he doesn't know what they are. He doesn't know if he's with them or against them. Outside, women with scarves on their heads wait in a long line. They hold brown-paper parcels tied with string. A truck pulls up. Trevor directs the unloading. Crates of eggs, clothes, paintings. They are going to sell the stolen goods. This is their link with the outside.

16.

One June, driving south from Canada, they encounter heat lightning after sunset. Some bolts jut horizontal across the sky; others rise and spread into jagged fingers. Jack has always believed lightning had to touch ground, but Trevor explains that the electrical current can move between clouds or between parts of the same cloud. The bolts that reach earth are sometimes eight miles long, but lightning that reaches between clouds can travel twenty to one hundred miles.

Jack is astonished that he's never noticed this before, lightning that shoots straight up or across the sky. It occurs to him that it might have been his father's fear, that lightning always struck the ground, struck houses, set dry fields ablaze. Jack and Trevor drive on in silence as light flashes and vibrates in the air around them.

17.

Once again, Jack wakes up in the beige hotel room. He's been napping after the prison dedication and before whatever it is that's planned for that evening. He's waiting for Trevor.

Jack thinks of the man he met walking beside Lake Geneva. He wishes he could hear again the story of how the man fell in love with his wife a second time, knowing all her faults. Jack longs to hear again how he thought he was going to her deathbed, and then she opened her eyes and smiled with half her mouth. He tries to picture Trevor on his deathbed, tries to imagine feeling for Trevor what the man in Geneva felt for his wife.

Jack remembers a woman he saw in the Frankfurt airport on their way back from Prague. She stood tall; the hood of her white robe partially covered her head. Because her hairline started so far back, she had an uncommonly long forehead. As she walked, her sons, daughters, and grandchildren flowed all around her. She moved with such majesty, he couldn't stop looking at her. Later, he found out she was part of a group of Somali refugees.

He was thinking about her on the plane waiting to leave Frankfurt for New York.

"He's cute, isn't he?" said Trevor.

"Who?"

"The steward," said Trevor. "Isn't that who you're staring at?"

Jack looked at Trevor, whose face wore a curious expression: lewd and playful and blank all at the same time. It seemed a face flung far from the man who wore it.

Jack thinks again, now, of the tribeswoman stepping through the crowd of Europeans like a queen, towering above them. He imagines her loosening her robe to let out parrots, ravens, bats, vultures, mice, hogs, camels, elephants, tigers, storms, sunbursts, boulders, all the rivers of the world.

He turns over, stares at the beige wall, thinks about the prison and its colors. He thinks about lightning that reaches between clouds, remembers his father putting out fires. He thinks about the prison dedication and the children whose voices he could not hear. He thinks about wanting to stop and sink—into sleep, into noise and squalor.

He closes his eyes. When Trevor returns to the room in ten minutes, Jack will get up, take two aspirin, call room service for a glass of milk to coat his stomach, so the cocktails won't catch him off guard. He will choose the right clothes, colors he's seen Trevor choose for himself a thousand times. He will dress, make the descent in the elevator, walk through the lobby, nod to the doorman, step into a limo or taxi or the car of some industrialist or government official, some dear friend of Trevor's, or one of Trevor's uncles.

But now he waits, his eyes still closed, and thinks he hears the children's voices after all, remembers moving his own lips without sound, thinks again of the goldfish opening and closing its mouth, as if to say "Yup … yup," its way of breathing, what he needs to do to stay alive.

ACKNOWLEDGMENTS

I'd like to thank the Helene Wurlitzer Foundation, the Virginia Center for the Creative Arts, and the Maine Arts Commission for their generous support in the form of fellowships and residencies. Special thanks to my students at the Maine College of Art, the Maine Writers and Publishers Alliance, the Salt Institute for Documentary Studies, Haystack Mountain School of Crafts and in independent retreats and workshops over the years for their courage and willingness to take risks, which always inspired my own.

A deep bow to my editor Karla Eoff.

People who have remained spirited friends of my writing life through the years include Gale Lawrence, Fritz Bell, Agnes Bushell, Kris Kleindienst, Sheila O'Connell, Monica Wood, Mary Bok, Charles Melcher, Bernie Meyers, Jamie Johnston, Jim Daniels, John Gilliss, Barrett Alexander, Harry Faddis, Jenny Uechi, and Linda Solomon Wood.

CPSIA information can be obtained at www.ICGtesting.com
Printed in the USA
LVOW06s1824310815

452226LV00021B/1272/P